Crewdley Times

NIG

Nig

This book is dedicated to Jennifer, Natasha, Keiran and Victoria.

1st edition 150 copies

STAR AND GARTER AGENCY & PUBLISHERS
18 Welch Gate
Bewdley
Worcs. DY12 2AT
Tel: 01299 402343

Printed by Veldonn Ltd, Kidderminster

British Library Cataloguing-in-Publication Date. A Catalogue record for this book is available.

Published 31st August 2016

ISBN 978-0-9562676-7.2

Star and Garter Books

(Established 1992)

Other books by Nigel Knowles still available from 'Star and Garter Publishers' are:

Those in Favour	ISBN 0.9519130.0X	£5.00
Observations Inside a Bewdley Ice-Cream Parlour	ISBN 0.9519130.18	£4.00
Identity Crisis	ISBN 0.9519130.2C	£4.00
Lord Lucan – The Letters of Sabrina (Out of Print)	ISBN 0.95191303.4	£5.00
Politics, Sex and Garlic Mushrooms	ISBN 0.9519130.4.2	£4.99
Bewdley 1762 – The Diary of Jack Nowles	ISBN 0.9519130.50	£4.00
Bewdley Parish Magazine 1886	ISBN 0.9519130.69	£6.99
American Revolution 1776 – Letters from New York, Boston and London	ISBN 0.9519130.77	£10.00
Bewdley Parish Magazine 1878-1880	ISBN 0.9519130.8.5	£10.00
De Gaulle and the Free French in Bewdley 1942-1944	ISBN 0.9519130.93	£12.00
Richard Baxter of Kidderminster	ISBN 0.9534704.07	£10.00
Kidderminster and Bewdley during the Civil War 1642-1651	ISBN 0.9534704.1.5	£12.00
The Mayor of Crewdley Exposed	ISBN 0.9534704.2.3	£5.00
Rowunda's problem is Arnold not me	ISBN 0.9534704.3.1	£5.00
Letters from Basra	ISBN 0.9534704.4.X	£2.00
Baldwin and De Gaulle, Bewdley 1942-1944- Diary of an Observer	ISBN 0.9534704.5.8	£10.00
Worcestershire – Seasons of the Earth	ISBN 0.9534704.7.4	£5.00
Bewdley, Ribbesford, Astley 1344-1944 – Waiting with the Owls	ISBN 0.9534704.6.6	£5.00
Bewdley and Kidderminster 1789 – Murder by Moonlight	ISBN 0.9534704.8.2	£5.00
Caractacus and the Bewdley Coracle	ISBN 978.0.9562676.0.3	£5.00
Crewdley Credit Crunch – An Update	ISBN 978.0.9562.676.1.0	£5.00
Bewdley Badgers, The Cats of Alcoutim and Spider and the Princess	ISBN 978.0.9562.676.2.7	£5.00
Four New Stage Plays: Baldwin - The Abdication: Bewdley Bayliff and the King: David Lloyd George - Criccieth to Ypres: A Touch of Wilde, Chekhov and Shaw	ISBN 978.0.9562676.3.4	£5.00
Two Stage Plays - "Liechtenstein" & "Knocking Doors"	ISBN 978.0.9562676.41	£10.00
Orson Welles Commits Magic	ISBN 978.0.9562.676.5.8	£10.00

Other plays by Nigel Knowles performed by Bewdley Original Theatre

"Knocking Doors" was performed at Bewdley Festival Fringe 2013
"Bewdley 4th August 1914 - Declaration of WW1", was performed in Jubilee Gardens, Bewdley on 4th August 2014 and at the Severn Centre, Highley, Shropshire, 7th November 2015

Star and Garter Books

(Est'd 1992)

Other books by Nigel Knowles still available from 'Star and Garter Publishers' are:

The Zennor Lantern, The Exile of D.H. Lawrence 1916-1917	ISBN 978.0.9562.676.6.5	£10.00
Crewdley Times	ISBN 978.0.9562.676.	£8.00

'The Zennor Lantern' won an open competition in the West Midlands in 2015 for an original play and was performed at The Courtyard Theatre, Hereford, and The Old Joint Stock Theatre Company, Birmingham, 2015.

'Baldwin - The Abdication' was performed at The Rose Theatre, Kidderminster in 2016.

In 1990 Heinemann published Nigel's 'The Tailors Dummy' in their New Writers Series.
"Letters from Basra" was a winning entry at a West Midlands Arts Forum in 2004.

To order any of the above books –

Write: Star and Garter Publishers, 18 Welch Gate, Bewdley, Worcs., DY12 2AT
Telephone: 01299 402343
Email: nigelknowlesbewdley@hotmail.com

To find out more information about books by Nigel Knowles and to order books, go to www.nigelknowlesbooks.co.uk

Also available at Amazon www.co.uk/books Nigel Knowles

CREWDLEY TIMES

Chapter 1

The Mayor was watching Liverpool versus Chelsea on his huge flat screen television in his Parlour at the Town Hall. His side was losing. He lit a cigar. His man, Anton Robespierre, pushed an ash tray across the table in preparation for the deluge of ash that would undoubtedly fall.

"Go and get fish and chips twice Robespierre", he instructed, "take the money from that syrup tin."

Robespierre sniffed loudly, approached the tin and breathed in sharply. "Does it have syrup in it?" he asked.

"No!" the Mayor answered, "it is in fact, a brilliantly disguised money box, guaranteed to fool all idiots like you."

"It does look good Your Worship", Robespierre clucked, "particularly with this packet of biscuits strategically placed next to it, with the knife and butter adding interest to an otherwise rather bland little corner of your Parlour."

The Mayor took his eyes off the TV to look hard at Robespierre, "Just take the lid off and get the money," he told him.

Robespierre obliged. "No syrup," he agreed. "What a surprise", the Mayor declared looking back at the television, "I should be at Wembley. It's always better to see the game live".

"Yes sir", said Robespierre, "except of course, they don't do fish and chips like ours in London."

"Point taken Robespierre," said the Mayor, "I'll have mushy peas and a pickled onion."

"Me too," Robespierre chirped, "cigar smoke and pickled onions – what a great smell!"

He was right of course. The Parlour would smell like a fish shop for the rest of the evening. Heaven was here then, in a two hundred year old building near the River Crewd in Worcestershire. No air – conditioning required, just an open window to let in the night air. The Mayor inhaled as Robespierre closed the door behind him. The Reds were still losing. He stared at the screen and a huge piece of ash fell onto the carpet as he blew rings of smoke in quick succession. "Does it have syrup in it?" he murmured, "typical!"

His team were not going to win, so like any fan worthy of the name, he switched off the TV.

Robespierre returned, fish and chips steaming from the newspaper packaging - last week's copy of the "The Weekly Weaver" – Crewdley's oldest and only tabloid of truth.

"You got the pickles and mushy peas?" the Mayor challenged his man.

"Absolutely", Robespierre replied.

"Right! Put 'em down on the desk- let's have 'em!"

They proceeded to devour their Civic Supper, washed down with Portuguese white wine and lager. The Mayor lay back in his chair and lit a large cigar. "Life is rich Robespierre," he said, "you can go now to your Quarters. Wake me at seven thirty with strong coffee."

"Yes sir", said Robespierre, "cigar smoke and the smell of fish and chips – heaven!"

The Mayor made his way to his bedroom and hit the sack. He was asleep before the light was out.

*

The body of the Mayor of Crewdley had been hanging from Crewdley Bridge for many weeks. His corpse was like a scarecrow, his clothes shredded, his face as blackened as the death mask on a dummy's head. His eyes were gone – pecked out by the crows and the gulls, as his corpse twisted on the rope in the river breeze beneath him. That it had come to this! The town's first citizen, hung by those same citizens after a mock trial worthy of those given to other tyrants who stole from the public purse and ran corrupt regimes – Ceachescue in Romania, Mussolini in Italy and yes – those aristocrats who bedevilled revolutionary France in 1789.

As the citizens walked over the bridge, many would spit where they knew the Mayor's body hung below. Others would drop cigarette butts and try to aim them to stick to his head or get them into the rags which were once a fine, dark suit of clothes. Youths would stone the corpse from the river bank and cheer the occasional hit. Catapults were fired at the ghoulish figure and by mistake, we assume, several fishing lines hung down from the body, cut free by fishermen who had whipped their baited lines into the corpse, and not the River Crewd. These now gave the appearance of the Mayor having been caught up in some kind of netting or wire fencing. But the gallows, still securely attached to the bridge parapets, dispelled any doubt. He had not fallen through a fence, or been caught up in netting. The Mayor of Crewdley had been hung! And Lord have mercy on his soul!

*

Harold Presbyterian shot up in bed from a deep sleep with these images in his head. He opened his eyes and felt the flesh on his arms, and most reassuringly, on his neck. "God!" he shouted, "that's the last time I have curry and tequila chasers! Robespierre - coffee!" But he hadn't had curry and tequila chasers, had he? How odd! He must have dreamt that as well? How odd – another element for Freudian study.

His aide-de-camp scuttled into the Mayoral bedchamber. "Yes your Worship – did you call?"

"Coffee!" he called again, "black- three sugars!"

Robespierre scuttled off towards the kitchen and the Mayor fell back onto his pillows. The image of his own corpse swinging in the breeze sent a shiver down his spine. The Mayor stared at the chandelier and then blinked.

"Coffee sir!" said Robespierre, "black with three sugars."

"Leave it on the table," said the Mayor, "and bring me my CD Player and the headphones".

Robespierre scooted out and closed the door behind him. "The English are weird," he said quietly to himself, "if you're going to listen to music, then at least let it fill the room!"

*

The Mayor was sitting in the front pew near the alter in St Crued's Church. He was spotted by the Reverend Wilfred Wooly who approached him with some caution. "Mr Mayor," he said quietly, "what a delightful surprise!"

"I have something to say to you", said the Mayor.

"Fire away", Wooly replied, "I'm all ears Your Worship".

"Not here," the Mayor replied, "in the Confessional box."

"My word!" exclaimed the Vicar of Crewdley, "I never imagined the day would come".

They walked slowly to the Confessional box – a handsome structure made from the finest English oak and embossed with beautiful carved figures of cherubs and angels, with oak leaves and barley corn, giving the impression of peace and tranquillity, once the defining image of the countryside which surrounded Crewdley and its church, that same church now surrounded on all sides by constant flows of traffic and youths on skateboards.

The Vicar drew back the heavy blue velvet curtain and stepped inside, taking the seat to the left, nearest the alter. It was most peculiar that Crewdley Church should have maintained this inherited feature from its Catholic past, but it had. A Church of England facility with a Catholic Confessional – the best of both worlds in a small English town where religious competition was once extremely fierce, and where churches still littered the little urban centre – C of E, Catholic, Methodist, Baptist, Quaker and several of the new evangelical churches where religious services seemed to revolve around the bashing of tambourines and yelling "Halleluiah!" at a disturbing level of decibels.

These new facilities were obviously not for the Mayor!

"Please come in", the Vicar said, holding back the curtain as he evinced his most stupid, supercilious grin. The Mayor took his seat and the Vicar drew the curtain. They sat in silence as candle smoke pervaded the Confessional box, causing it to resemble the Smoke Room of a Public House before the ban.

Each was now separated from the other by a superb, hand carved oak grill which allowed only a dimmed image of each person for the other to see.

"I want you to come to my side", said the Mayor.

"I beg your pardon?" answered the Vicar.

"Come on man! I haven't got all day – come around here and sit down".

"Most irregular Mr Mayor", said Wooly, "it goes against all custom and practice."

"Zip it!" the Mayor said sternly, "just do it".

So the Vicar eased his way next to the Mayor and sat down. "How can I help?" he asked.

"Well, if it were just a question of you and I – man to man – then obviously you couldn't". The Mayor stared at his man and the Vicar's lip quivered.

"Oh dear", he sighed, "have I done something to displease you?"

"No more than usual", said the Mayor, "but this matter is not just you and I, man to man. It's more than that. It's to do with conscience".

"Oh really?" the Vicar retorted.

"Yes! And it's to do with confession".

"Goodness me!" the Vicar exclaimed with surprise, "I can't believe what I'm hearing".

"That's just the point", the Mayor told him, "you are not going to hear anything. Put these headphones on and press that button on the player. You are going to listen to Elgar whilst I have a chat with whoever it is who listens in on these occasions. Just think of yourself as being here in body but not in spirit as I have a little chat with something that knows all and says nothing."

Wooly put the headphones on and pressed the button on the player. Elgar filled his head and the Mayor mouthed a few stern words that Wooly couldn't hear. This process only lasted for a minute or so, then the Mayor pressed the button and Elgar ceased.

"I quite enjoyed that", said Wooly.

"I'm going to give you five thousand pounds for the church fund", said the Mayor, "and you can put it down as Anonymous Donor".

"My word!" said Wooly, "we can start to repair the clock tower".

"If you wish", the Mayor replied, "better still, take those bells down! They disturb me every Sunday morning".

"Sorry Mr Mayor, I couldn't do that".

"Pity", he replied, "I'll just have to carry on listening to Elgar instead".

Wooly passed him the headphones and player, again adopting his stupid grin.

"Get a grip Wooly!" the Mayor snapped, "you're losing the plot!" He drew the curtain and made his exit, leaving Wooly still seated in the Confessional box. "I wonder what he said? "he queried, looking at the bag of money he had been given, "God moves in very mysterious ways indeed!"

*

"Redemption", the Mayor uttered quietly as he walked along the river bank, "ridiculous!" He continued to walk rather slowly, enjoying the quietness and beauty of the place. "

"David Hockney my arse", he muttered, reflecting on the great man's London exhibition, already trailed several times for the viewing public on TV. "Yorkshire my arse!", then louder, causing a swan to take flight, "Worcestershire is the place! Come to Crewdley Hockney – if you dare! You'd need Michelangelo on your shoulder to capture this little lot!"

He stumbled on – along the dirt river bank path, stepping over tree roots and brambles, looking at the fields to his left and the river to his right as he walked away from Crewdley – or God's Holy City as a little man in a flat cap had loudly announced to all of the passengers on a bus, including, on that occasion, the Mayor himself, given that his Rolls Royce was temporarily kaput. The bus had been approaching the bridge and obviously, the little man wanted there to be no doubt in passengers minds that they were indeed, about to cross the bridge into Crewdley. The Mayor had never seen the man before that event, or since. "Very odd", he reflected as a horse walked towards him up to the fence. The horse looked at the Mayor and the Mayor looked at the horse.

"Good morning", said the Mayor to the animal, "do you realise that in a past life, you were probably a Senator in Caligula's Rome?" The horse gave no indication that it did, and the Mayor walked on.

He saw a large copse of trees across a field, leant against a fence and sniffed. He knew what the trees hid from the view of all, except the most inquisitive. The grass was wet on the gentle slope up to the oaks and sycamores, but it had been cut. He looked for a minute or two. No cattle, particularly no wild bulls which could stamp a man into the ground – even a Mayor, and even without his red flowing robe trimmed with ghastly animal furs that were enough to send blood hounds howling and fox hounds barking mad.

He climbed over the stile and began his walk to the trees, still looking both ways just in case a bull was loose and he had to scramble back. It was all clear – two hundred yards up the slope, through a part-broken Victorian iron gate, then into the trees.

It was spooky – no life, no birds, just the cold wind gushing through the dark trees with their long, deep shadows that made it seem as if dawn would never break. He checked his watch – noon and still dark in this lost place.

The Mayor saw the grave stones protruding through the brambles and the ivy. The head stones were covered with moss and stained dark green from the long years of being showered with rain from the tangled canopy of trees and the absence of sunlight.

He looked at a gravestone that he could actually get close enough to read the inscription on ...."Here lies the body of .... who departed this life 16th September 1862." He went to others - men and women, young and old – all long gone. Tax payers once. And here they lay in honest graves, a facility denied to tax cheat and ultra sinner Al Capone, after his quick-lime eradication in Alcatraz, the sinner's Cathedral.

The Mayor stumbled on and saw the ruined brick building that had once been a church. He approached it with care. No fear of wild bulls in here, but what about wild dogs, or even worse - wild men and women? No – he looked in through the broken door way – just graffiti and empty whisky bottles. Pathetic in every sense. A church with no roof, nor door, nor windows - brambles growing up through the floor – pathetic.

He edged his way out and walked back through the trees. He saw the thing for which he had really come to look at again after so many years. The monument to a long-dead Town Clerk of Crewdley, Mr Joseph Lacey. Born 8th April 1802 died 27th July 1896 ...... son of James and Elizabeth....... plantation owners of Jamaica ..... Justice of the Peace .... RIP.

The Mayor reflected on the edifice and its statements of fact.

"Jamaica", he mumbled, "Town Clerk of Crewdley............ no doubt a formidable opponent."

*

The Mayor retraced his footsteps back through the trees, across the field onto the river path, and finally into Riverside West. He walked slowly onto Crewdley Bridge and stared down at the river. Celts, Romans, Vikings and Anglo-Saxons – had all come up here in their river boats. Men had paddled coracles for hundreds, probably thousands of years.

Trows had been pulled up and down the river by men and horses, journeys taking wool, cloth, carpets, coal animals, iron ware, pewter etc, to Worcester, Gloucester, Bristol and beyond.
The so –called Golden Age had been the 18th century, before the roads and canals and the railways. He looked at the water – it was timeless. The river cut through Crewdley like a living artery, giving life and solace to its citizens.
"Canals my arse", he mumbled, then walked back down across the bridge into Church Street, and then into the Town Hall. He used the back door to get into his own house, "Plantation owners in Jamaica", he said to himself, "and got washed up in Crewdley."

*

Preston Peters was on automatic pilot. His fingers were hitting the computer pad, words were indeed coming up on the screen. But his brain was not in gear ...... Wedding Anniversary celebrated in style ......guests all wore yellow to remind the happy couple they had first met on the production line of a butter factory in Worcestershire ..... guests entertained by ukulele trio ....etc, etc, etc.
And this was the hub of the "Weekly Weaver", the very epicentre of journalistic activity in Crewdley. Things never change! Well alright – new technology had been introduced - the computers!

But, according to Peters, Crewdley was the equivalent of a cultural desert, a news-free zone in which absolutely nothing newsworthy ever happened.
"What's happening out there on the streets"? Archibald McSnadden asked him sharply.
"Nothing!" answered Peters.
"Why not?"
"Because nothing ever does."
"I strongly suggest you go out and find something worthy of your salary," said McSnadden. "We haven't been the news centre of Crewdley life for a hundred and fifty years by having nothing to say. Wedding reports don't cut the mustard."
"Well – at least we are not on trial for phone hacking," Peter's declared "and I haven't been through the Mayor's dustbin looking for evidence of corruption."
"Your problem is you don't think outside the box," said the Editor.

"I think I've probably reached the zenith of my career," said Peters, "it's possible I've found my comfort zone – weddings, funerals, fetes, court sessions – that's about it, eh chief?"
"You need an ambition transplant", said McSnadden, "our readers want excitement – intrigue – sentiment – scoops!"
"In Crewdley?" asked Peters, "it would be a shame to wake them – don't you think chief? A hundred and fifty years of pap and then a front page worthy of the gutter-press. It ain't gonna happen."
"Never say never", McSnadden said firmly, as if he knew it was only a question of time before the news-dam burst and Crewdley was swept away in a deluge of shock and scandal – all delivered in a single issue of "The Weekly Weaver", available at all local Newsagents (both of them).
"Ok chief", Peters replied, "in the meantime, what was the name of that butter factory in Kidderminster where the happy couple met? I just want to really spice this wedding anniversary story up a few notches – you know – from incredibly boring to just boring."
"The Co-op", McSnadden told him, "he was the manager and she worked on the production line".
"So he didn't work on the production line?" queried Peters.
"No!"
"Oh! I'd better make that clear", said Peters.
"Yes", said McSnadden, "people have very long memories around here. They would flood the letters pages for weeks telling us we'd got it wrong. That wedding was only fifty years ago. Half the population were probably present at the service".
"It's a small world," remarked Peters.
"Indeed it is", answered McSnadden, "so when you've finished the wedding anniversary story, why don't you have a look around the town for a story? Riverside East is usually a bed of intrigue".
"Pardon?"
"Just joking", said McSnadden, looking over Peter's shoulder to his computer, "two 't's' in butter", he declared, "you're losing the plot! One 't' in Plot".
"Thank you chief – two 't's butter, one 't' plot – thanks!"

*

Preston Peters wandered aimlessly along the riverside, looking at the river Crewd as it meandered its way through the town. He saw Robespierre walking towards him. He watched as the Mayor's man stopped and went to the railings. Robespierre threw pieces of bread down to the ducks, geese and swans which were paddling about near to the steps.
As the bread hit the water, the birds were joined by a host of seagulls. These birds were the new arrivals in town. Robespierre took a step back as the gulls screeched and dived for the bread.
"You shouldn't feed them bread", said Peters.
"Why not?" asked Robespierre.
"It's not good for them", the reporter answered.
"The Mayor eats it", declared Robespierre.
"He should try wholemeal bread – he would eat more of it – less waste".
"The Mayor is not a health-food person", Robespierre told him.
"Why doesn't that surprise me?" Peters called out over the screeching and quacking, "anyway – what's happening in Crewdley politics Robespierre?"
Robespierre threw his last crust and faced his inquisitor. "All is well within the Council", he declared.
"Oh really?"

“Absolutely!” Robespierre said as emphatically as he could whilst being dive-bombed by the birds.
“Well I heard there was a problem”, Peters lied.
Robespierre looked at Peters and walked off. Peters continued to look down into the water and called out loudly, “Have a nice day!”

*

Eccentricity in Crewdley is nothing new. There are many individuals who would be considered eccentric by the normal standards of behaviour. However, Rupert Beard, brother of the Town Clerk Bernard, could perhaps claim the title of Crewdley’s finest example of English eccentricity – not that he ever would, because to him, the rest of the Crewdley population were the odd ones out.
But let us consider the question at issue. Rupert Beard was a man of independent financial means who liked to keep a low profile. Rumour had it that his inclination had been brought about by either a) his attempt to evade the tax man, b) his flight from an over –eager divorcee, c) his absolute refusal to mix in social society, d) his desire to live rent-free at someone else’s expense.

Whatever the reason had been, the fact remained that Rupert Beard had lived (rent free) in the garden of the Vicarage, in a tepee for many years. Wilfred Wooly, Vicar of Crewdley, himself no stranger to eccentric behaviour, had exercised Christian charity to a soul in dire need of refuge. His wife Winifred would not have opened the door to Beard, but Crewdley’s religious conscience had, on this occasion, over-ruled her.

The gentleman had become part of the fixtures and fittings of the Vicarage. His tent was pitched in the corner of the garden near the wall. It was not the only item of interest that had been placed on the garden lawn. A set of 18th century stocks testified to a most rough and ready system of justice that was to have been had in Crewdley in days of yor. Worse still, a ducking stool rested beneath a magnolia tree. Witch trials, hangings for horse stealing - deportation for trade union activity, then in later more enlightened times, jail for minor theft and birching for naughty children. All now, almost forgotten, except for the wooden artefacts that sullied the Vicar’s garden.
So here was where Rupert Beard hung his hat – or more precisely, his head-dress of turkey, feathers which he wore quite regularly. He rarely went out in the streets. If he did, it was usually at night to go to the Co-op or walk by the river. He slept on a pile of animal skins in his tent – sheep wool, cow hides and one or two blankets given to him by the Woolys. They also provided him with much of his food. They also bought him his clothes – charity shops mostly, with the occasional discarded pair of shoes or old jacket that Wilfred had grown tired of.
So how did Rupert Beard spend his time in his tepee? Rupert wrote! Copious amounts actually - all paper and pen – long hand – no computers or type writers, just biros and free pens that the Woolys got from magazines and businesses looking for business.
Exactly what he wrote was unknown, even to the Woolys. His papers were stored in a very large trunk which took up quite some space in his tent. Ah! The English at work and play! Robespierre considered them all mad whether they lived in tents or not.

*

Without wishing to bore any observer of life in Crewdley, it would be remiss not to mention several other people in the lexicon of eccentricity. Percy Fish, at first glance, particularly if he were seen out on his own, would hardly seem to qualify as eccentric. However, Percy needed to be seen “in the round” as it were. He was barely ever alone.

Percy was one of those people who didn't give a damn about appearances or social grace. That is why he kept a pig! Pongo and Percy were regular features of Crewdley life. Percy kept Pongo on a lead and walked the pig through the streets of Crewdley – usually up along Dark Street and into the forest to hunt for truffles. Percy spoke to the pig as if it were human. There is no evidence to suggest Percy ever expected an answer in English.

However, there was an almost psychic understanding between pig and man. The pig seemed to get it. Over many years, there had no doubt been many pigs, but all were called Pongo. His sense of smell was uncanny, especially when grubbing for truffles. Percy kept him in an outhouse in his garden. A well-fed pig is a happy pig and Pongo was extremely well fed. Many neighbours gave Percy food for his trotter, and the pig had long ago been accepted as a member of Crewdley society, albeit the underclass of society, if not exactly of the proletariat, then perhaps as a pig-letariat or pork-letariat. The neighbours esteem extended so far as to sending Pongo cards at Christmas.

Percy decided that Pongo's birthday was 1st May. So some of the children gave him birthday cards – usually with pigs on and never in bad taste depicting a butchers shop or a pan of bacon. Percy was content- not rich nor even well off –just content. Long may it be so!

The next candidate for inclusion in the list of Crewdley eccentrics was, alas, the Vicar himself. Wilfred Wooly had a predilection to dress up in deer skins, don an antler set and run through Crewdley forest, bellowing, rutting and calling the deer herd to listen up because the king stag was amongst them.

Oh dear! Periods of incarceration in "health farms" and quiet Manor Houses in the country had failed to quell his Paganism. Winifred merely lived from one week to the next with the fear that Wilfred would once again revert to type. Such can be the pressure brought about on leading members of the Church of England in a period of religious decline in a decadent capitalist society. Forgiveness is a virtue. Long may it be so!

*

Finally, for now, we need to consider the Sisters Flack- Dorothy and Myrtle – two spinsters who strike fear into Anton Robespierre and others, just by being there. These two English ladies are considered bonkers by most. Their wool shop is considered a front for gambling, the import and export of drugs and guns, a safe haven for the Mafia and a place of inequity and depravity. A wool shop is what it ain't! Long may it be so!

*

This then, is the list of Crewdley eccentrics. Other citizens have personalities which are peculiar. Robespierre himself is peculiar. He is unable and unwilling to escape his past. His ancestor changed sides at the Battle of Waterloo in 1815 and made his way to Crewdley. Yet give or take one or two Anglo-French dispositions, Robespierre is not really an eccentric. A vassel of the Mayor's – yes! A fool –yes! A sucker for attractive young women (barmaids particularly) – yes! But not eccentric in the classical English tradition of a Percy Fish, a Wilfred Wooly or, heaven forbid – the Flack sisters.

If Robespierre was peculiar, it was widely acknowledged that the Mayor was single – minded, ambitious, vindictive, a womaniser, a formidable political operator on a small town scale; arrogant, a bully, a man who put Crewdley first, because he was the Mayor and his greed for political power and economic security put him well above the rest of would-be politicos in this unique town on the banks of the River Crewd.

Yes indeed – Harold Presbyterian controlled Crewdley like a shepherd controls his sheep – baaa!

Long may it be so!

*

"So what have you got for me?" asked McSnadden.
"Nothing chief", admitted Preston Peters, "it's as quiet as a church yard out there".
"Huh! No wonder the Canary Wharf mob considered phone tapping as part of their job description. Instead of doing the Times crossword, it was hacking into emails and bank accounts."

"Ah! You are referring to the Crewdley Credit Crunch chief," Peters declared with a degree of alacrity and alarm, "bad wasn't it?"
"We're not out of it yet laddie," said McSnadden, "but I am not advocating phone tapping or email hacking – I'm just bemoaning the fact that we can't get a good story from anywhere in this town."
Peters stared at his computer, "Sorry chief," he said, "I'll tell you what though – the council is decking out the road island on the by-pass; lots of flowers, a new sign post indicating the through route to Crewdley – that kind of thing".
"A contradiction in terms," said McSnadden, "what's the point in having a by-pass if the council puts up a sign saying this way to Crewdley? The thing about a by-pass is that traffic avoids the town!"
"Good point chief," Peters declared, "when is a by-pass not a by-pass chief?"
"What are you talking about boy?"
"When it's a heart by-pass. Get it chief?"

*

The Mayor was still brooding about the monument in the trees to the late Town Clerk.
"Bloody cheek," he mumbled, "Town Clerk – massive monument – forty five Mayors – nothing."
He poured himself another glass of wine and closed his eyes. The figure of the Corpse – his Corpse – was still swinging from the bridge.
"Robespierre!" he yelled, "more cigars – pronto!"

*

At face value, the Mercian Bank seemed to be almost over the recent Credit Crunch, the Government having bailed it out with a hundred or so billion pounds being put into the banking system.
But a worsening of the Euro crisis or a crash in New York could yet precipitate the shutters going down on Crewdley's only banking institution. However, the new manager, Mrs Croker, had a tight grip on all monetary matters affecting Crewdley investors and borrowers. She still missed Roland Jones, her predecessor, but her new position had given her more financial security. However, Mrs Croker kept a picture of the one that got away in a drawer in her office desk. If candles had been allowed in the workplace, she would have lit one for him. But things had moved on, and we find her now reading through the columns of "Men Seeking Women" in "The Weekly Weaver." ...."Good looking man wants to meet attractive woman. Age not so important as having a friendly and out-going personality. I am middle aged, a theatre goer and financially independent. Telephone 04963 224018."
Mrs Croker closed the pages; ...."I might just try that number."
She did. The phone rang out. "Hello," she said, "I'm responding to your number in the newspaper."
She waited for an answer. Finally, a frightened man said, "Sorry – you've got the wrong number, "and he put the phone down.
"What's the matter Robespierre?" asked the Mayor, "you've gone as white as a bed sheet."
"Mrs Croker," he stammered, "I recognised her voice."
"So you put the phone down on her?"
"Yes," said Robespierre.

"Excellent! Do you want to tell me why?"
"No!"
"Your telephone style is not the best. You still have some way to go before you qualify as competent. Why did she ring your mobile?"
"I don't know," he lied, "wrong number."
"Don't ever take up poker," the Mayor told him, "look at you! Nervous as a dodgy dentist – perspiring, even your hands are shaking. If I ever see you in a casino – you're fired!"
"Yes sir – you won't!" said Robespierre, "I'm not a gambler."
The Mayor stared hard at his man. "You've been putting adverts in the Lonely Hearts Club column again, haven't you?"
Robespierre jumped to attention. "Yes sir! Do you want my resignation?"
"No," the Mayor told him, "I thought you were still knocking around with that barmaid Sharon Hayes? What's up? Has she given you the push?"
"She has a young boyfriend Mr Mayor," answered Robespierre.
"Has he got money?"
"No sir," Robespierre replied.
"She'll be back," the Mayor said, "but just make sure Mrs Croker never gets to find your telephone number. Mind you, even she would say you were not the article described on the tin. What did you put – dashing young man wants to meet attractive blond?"
"No sir – I was most conservative in my description."
"You've just had a very narrow escape Robespierre. So let that be a lesson to you. Always see the intended object of desire in the flesh, else you could both be fatally shocked – get me an omelette and we'll share a bottle of Crewdley blanc," said the Mayor, "you really ought to know better at your age."

Robespierre stood at ease. His boss was clever. He should stick with him and ignore the lure of any passing femme fatale.
"An omelette sir, straight away," he said, wondering of course what Sharon Hayes was doing and who she was with. No fool like an old fool and Robespierre was fully qualified in that department.

*

Chapter 2

The Mayor was still obsessed with three facets of his life in June 2012. The first was Redemption – his attempt to make right that for which he had done wrong in the past – a hopeless cause; his clumsy attempt to buy his way into the church's good books was dependent upon Wilfred Wooly propagating the Mayor's case – a truly futile prospect, but Wooly was still the Vicar of Crewdley. No – the man was useless and worse. So the Mayor's donation was really between him and, well himself.
His second obsession was that ghastly recurring dream involving his Corpse and the bridge. Obviously, there was more to this than was first apparent. He would have to hope that, over time, his sleep would not be disturbed by such an awful spectre.

The third thing, he liked. Well if not liked, then he was keen to wrestle with the phenomenon of The Late Rich and Powerful Town Clerk. It set his imagination racing .... Joseph Lacey 8th April 1802 died 27th July 1896 .... son of James and Elizabeth .... Plantation owners of Jamaica .... Justice of the Peace .....RIP. He knew all about Town Clerks. The first point was, Town Clerks are not elected – a weakness in any battle for the soul of the populace in a democracy like Crewdley's. But someone like Lacey would no doubt have stuck to the civic business of the riverside town like an old, encrusted barnacle. He would have seen Mayors come and go. And a Justice of the Peace too. The Mayor knew the sort. Fortunately Bernard Beard, Crewdley's own TC (seventh generation) was no threat at all. There would be no monument to Bernard Beard. But to Harold Presbyterian? In an economic down turn? With a discontented electorate? Stranger things have happened - never say never, but the Mayor was not optimistic. Anyway – tonight he would visit Mrs Pippa Munroe, his mistress and headmistress of Crewdley High School.
"Just keep the Rolls on the Quayside," he said to Robespierre, "I might fancy a drive out into the forest later on."
"After midnight?" Robespierre enquired, "it's a school day tomorrow. Mrs Monroe needs her sleep."
"You cheeky little tic!" said the Mayor, "anymore comments like that and I'll tell Mrs Croker it was you she was ringing."
"Sorry Mr Mayor," said Robespierre, "of course I shall wait outside 'Caspian House' for you to emerge – singly or together."
"You still don't quite get English, do you Robespierre?"
"French is in my blood sir," Robespierre answered.
"Yes – so don't forget the Guillotine. It's always an option for an angry mob, even an English mob," said the Mayor. Just then, a cold draught came in from the open window and caused the Mayor to shiver.
"Brrmm," he brrmmd, "if you ever see a wooden gallows on Crewdley Bridge, walk quickly by," he said.
"Yes sir – I shall," Robespierre assured him, saying quietly under his breath, "the English are mad."

*

The Flack's Wool Shop was a throw-back to the 1950's. No fluorescent lights, no buzzers under mats that let the owners know a customer had wandered in. No modern shelving – dark English oak sufficed. An old fashioned till stood on the counter – again an oak boarding system polished to perfection. And not for the Flacks that scourge of modern shopping – piped music! However, Brittany Baxter, the émigré from The Mercian Bank, was a modern attraction in every way. It will be recalled that Brittany was transferred to the Wool Shop as a method of getting her out of the way of Roland Jones – the Manager who left in a hurry. To her credit, Brittany had slotted into the ways of the Wool Shop extremely well.

Many young men, and older ones, brought new business to this Emporium of Exotic Commerce. Sales went up by tens of thousands in percentage value, notwithstanding that the starting position of the Flack's woollen business account was very, very modest. Yet now, she had apparently mastered the wool trade! The nuances of angora and the joy of knitting scarves, gloves, socks, cardigans, skirts, stockings, polo jumpers – all were in her gift, carefully explained to hoards of young men who suddenly became customers. Brittany always wore red – the Flack sisters usually wore black. There could be absolutely no mistake as to who had served whom.

One of the key factors in Brittany's decisiveness to transfer from the bank to the Wool Shop, was her love of the shop cat – Claws. Another factor was that Brittany considered the Flacks were normal and nice. Dorothy and Myrtle actually liked Brittany. She was attractive, they were not! She was young they were old. She was out- going they were secretive. She was happy and they were suspicious, she was pleasant and they were weird.

A business partnership it was not, but a working relationship it was. The Flacks, of course, had no offspring to leave the business too.

Who cared? The Mayor would have been glad to have seen the Flacks go under in the Crewdley Credit Crunch. But they had hung on, defying all monetary and social logic. The Black Arts indeed cause much consternation and surprise to those not directly involved in the Wool Trade.

The Mayor had wondered if the Flacks had been propped up by venture capitalists – Warren Buffet, Richard Branson, Alan Sugar? And rumours persisted that two Italian gentlemen were frequent visitors to The Wool Shop. Luigi and Salvatori were not names usually associated with the Crewdley wool trade. And yet, their names were on record as being overnight guests at "The Forest Hotel."

*

Preston Peters had no idea what was going on and neither did his editor Archibald McSnadden. For them, The Wool Shop was not even a blip on the radar. The Mayor always suspected the Flacks were at the very centre of something bigger than Crewdley. Robespierre was scared stiff of the Flacks. They conjured up terrifying spectres of ghouls, ghosts –even goblins, to this man of Paris.

"Go and see what the Flacks are up to," the Mayor told him, "it's too quiet. Go in and buy a ball of wool."

"Sir!" he retorted, "I fear for my safety!"

"Don't be stupid Robespierre. Two little old ladies can't hurt you."

"It was little old ladies who sat at the steps of Madame Guillotine when they beheaded the Aristocrats in 1789," Robespierre spluttered,

"You are not an Aristocrat!" said the Mayor, "take a couple of quid from the syrup tin – I'm feeling generous - now beat it!"

Robespierre did as he was told. He got to the shop door, turned the handle and went inside. No one was there. He walked slowly up to the counter. Still no one. Suddenly, Myrtle Flack shot up from the bowels of the earth like a ghoul rising on a trap door from a grave.

"Yes – what is it?" she said.

Robespierre jumped, "My God! Every time I come in here you nearly give me a heart attack!"

"So don't come in," she advised, "what do you want Robespierre? I suppose the Mayor sent you – as usual."

"No!" he lied, "I want a ball of wool."

"What colour?" she enquired, with the innocence of a novice Nun.

"Blue!"

"Well I'm not going to sell you any," Myrtle declared with a finality that was definitely final.
"Oh!" Robespierre gasped, "before saying again, "Oh!"
"Good morning", she said, "watch out for the cat. I don't want him to go outside just at the moment. He's just caught a mouse and I don't want him disturbed."
Robespierre backed away from the counter, as if Myrtle Flack was a Royal and he a Serf retreating in abject deference. He turned to face the door, shuddered, and went out.
"Idiot!" said Myrtle, "Brittany – could you make me a cup of tea please? And I'll have a biscuit."

*

Seamus McGurk was arm –wrestling a customer in "The Star and Garter". He flattened the man's arm onto the table and laughed loudly, "That'll cost 'yer!" he shouted, "double or quits."
"It's ok", said the man, "I can't afford time off work. I just thought I'd catch you in an unguarded moment."
"That'll be the day," shouted McGurk, "if I start losin' to the loiks of you."
The man put his jacket on and left the pub. McGurk strutted around like John Wayne, "Is there anybody else who'd like to troi a bit of arm wrestlin' wi me fer a free drink?"
There were no takers. "What about you Robespierre?" he shouted, "you get all that exercise carryin' the Mayor's Mace."
"No thank you Mr McGurk," said Robespierre. "I don't mind a game of bowls, but I'm not equipped for arm-wrestling – thanks for asking."
The customers carried on drinking. Robespierre resumed his seat and looked across the bar room to Sharon Hayes. He went to join her. "Where is your young man Sharon?" he asked.
"I dumped him," she answered, looking as attractive as ever, in spite of chewing gum and filing her nails.
"Oh good," said Robespierre, "let me buy you a drink."
"Double vodka", she said without emotion, "and I think I'll have a cheese sandwich."
"Certainly," Robespierre said with some excitement, "but it's your night off. What are you doing in here?"
"Waiting for you Anton," she said curtly.
"How wonderful," he answered, "we could go for a Chinese after."

*

Dorothy and Myrtle Flack were sitting quietly in the living room at the back of "The Wool Shop" listening to the radio. Claws the cat was curled up in front of the grate. It was the 1st July and just about warm enough to endure and enjoy the English climate without a coal fire being lit. However, April, May and June had been the wettest and coldest on record and the cat was obviously feeling the cold. The fire would not be lit on principle, irrespective of the calendar date. The Flacks were drinking cups of soup, the cat stretched out a paw, but gave no other sign of life.
Myrtle began to knit with a ball of red wool. Dorothy did the same, but chose blue.
"I'm going to knit a little red football shirt for teddy," said Myrtle.
"Ah yes! I thought I'd knit a blue one," said Dorothy.
"Great minds think alike!" they said together, "I'm going to put Spain on mine in yellow letters," announced Myrtle, "I shall probably, do the shirt with long arms rather than short. It will make more of a splash."
"I'd better do the same," declared Dorothy, "I'll do Italy in white letters on the back."
"Excellent," said Myrtle, "no need to rush, the game hasn't started yet."

And so the Ladies of the Night began to knit. Claws seemed fascinated, but made no attempt to catch the wool. "There's a good cat," Myrtle said, "save yourself for catching mice."

*

Robespierre had bought Sharon Hayes several vodkas in "The Star and Garter" and she was rather loud as she knocked them back. "Hey Seamus!" she shouted, "have you been watering the drinks down?"
McGurk was pulling a pint. "Hark at her!" he shouted back, "the barmaid who gives away the secrets of the trade!"
"I tell you what Seamus!" she yelled, "give us another fizzy water – oops sorry! Another double vodka- Robespierre's paying – aren't you Anton?"
Robespierre went to the bar, " And I'll have the same," he said, putting down a ten pound note, "and have one yourself Mr McGurk."
"Oi will," he said, "and that will be another fiver.
Robespierre paid up and took the drinks. The course of true love does not run smooth. Sharon took the vodka and knocked it back in one swig.
Robespierre checked his wallet. "Would you like to come back to my flat?" he asked her.
"Wha' for?" she spluttered.
"Romance," he said.
"Get lost Robespierre."
Reluctantly, Robespierre drank up and walked towards the door.
"Take her with yuh Robespierre!" bellowed McGurk.
"I'm stopping in here!" she retaliated, "I want to serve behind the bar!"
"Come back tomorrow Sharon," he said, "you'd be givin' the drinks away- here – take a tenner with you on yer way out." He stuck the note in her hand and she staggered to the door.
Robespierre held her up and they went outside.
"The night is young," he said.
"Well you're not, "she yelled," I want another drink."
"Let's go up to the Mayor's Parlour," he suggested, "he's got vodka and champagne."
"I don't want that stuff – the bubbles go up my nose!" said Sharon.
They made their way unsteadily to the Town Hall and up to the Mayor's Parlour.
"I've got the key," said Robespierre, as Sharon Hayes wobbled about on her high heels. Robespierre opened the door and Sharon fell in. He scrambled after her. "Oh my God!" he said in terror, as he saw the near-naked bodies of Crewdley's most eminent couple.
"Robespierre!" shouted the Mayor, "you little toad! How dare you! Get out! And take this woman with you!"
Sharon Hayes rolled on the carpet and laughed, "Bloody hell- excuse me," she slurped, "he told me we were going in the betting shop."
Pippa Monroe grabbed a coat from the back of a chair and covered herself. "You termite Robespierre!" the Mayor yelled, "it's a good job that woman won't be able to remember this tomorrow!"
"But I shall," said Mrs Monroe, "I think you had better take me home Harold. It's getting late!"
Robespierre somehow managed to get Sharon Hayes to her feet, and they stumbled down the stairs. The Mayor and Mrs Pippa Monroe got dressed, and after regaining as much composure as was possible, he walked her home to "Caspian House". A night to forget. But alas for Robespierre, it would not be forgotten.

A bizarre Sunday night in Crewdley – a quiet time in the Wool Shop, a cauldron of football in Kiev and a rather defining moment in the Mayor's Parlour. Who would have rather been where? Robespierre would have preferred Kiev, but beggars can't be choosers.

*

At 8am precisely, Robespierre took a mug of tea into the Mayor who was still in bed. He placed it on the side table. The Mayor was reading a book.
"Good morning Mr Mayor," Robespierre said expressing as little emotion and fear in his voice as possible. The Mayor remained silent.
"Oh dear," muttered Robespierre, "have I offended you in anyway Your Worship?"
"Are you insane?" the Mayor asked him, "you crash into my Parlour – unannounced - and drunk!"
"No sir!" Robespierre insisted, "I was sober."
"You allow that woman to roll around the floor – drunk!"
"No sir – she was sober!"
"Robespierre!"
"Yes sir?"
"You took Sharon Hayes into my Parlour."
"Errm – we thought no one would be in at that time sir."
"People were in!"
"Ah yes - but Sharon will have forgotten by now, I shall tell her we went into the betting shop."
"At midnight!"
"She won't remember Your Worship – she never does!"
"That's not the point! My inner sanctum – my personal private place – tarnished now by the picture of you and that barmaid crashing in to commit something beyond normal comprehension."
"I just wanted to take her for a night cap sir," said Robespierre, now beginning to quiver, "it was no more than that – just an innocent late night drink."
"It's the Mayor's Parlour you little shit! Not the games room in "The Star and Garter."
"I'm in love!" said Robespierre.
"Get yourself checked into a Psychiatric Unit. You're mental faculties have left you. She is a disaster and you will end up on the scrap heap."
"You don't approve?" Robespierre asked stupidly.
"You can't afford The Priory, so I suggest you see Doc Hargreaves as a first step."
"My mind is as clear as a bell sir," said Robespierre.
"Never that," said the Mayor, "you're brain has gone – you're wits have gone and you're money has probably gone."
"I've got my savings sir," Robespierre told him, "Sharon just likes a good time."
"With you? You're three times her age - Ah! Wait a minute! I've got it! You realise that and that's why you put that advert in Lonely Hearts!"
"Just an experiment sir. I just thought I'd see what happened - perhaps a new beginning? But when Mrs Croker telephoned – I lost my nerve. And so I have reverted to Sharon. With her I feel I am on safe ground."
"Safe ground! You are in an earthquake zone."
"Perhaps shaky sir – but not an earthquake. Sharon is a little volatile and sometimes causes a bit of a scene."
"Last night's performance was beyond the pale. Take her with you when you check into the clinic."

"She is young sir – high spirits", said Robespierre with feigned enthusiasm.
"Not high spirits – white spirits – vodka!" said the Mayor, "she will be preserved better than Tutankhamen, I warn you Robespierre, young women like her are not for you."
"But you pursued Brittany Baxter," said Robespierre, "and she and Sharon are the same age."
"How dare you! Do not presume to compare yourself to me!"
"No sir!"
"Brittany Baxter was a mere interlude – not an opera! Where is your dignity?"
"Somewhere near the bar at "The Star and Garter". Sharon and I were lovers in previous lives – probably in Revolutionary France."
"Rubbish!"
"It's possible Your Worship. And I think the Flacks have been here before."
"My God - not that! Fate could not inflict such a travesty on such a small community as Crewdley."
"Oh yes sir – Crewdley in the 17th Century - during the Civil War! I see them as witches burnt at the stake by Oliver Cromwell. I see their Wool Shop as a spiders web of black magic. They were put on trial for ruining the harvest. Their cat is probably directly descended from a Scottish wild cat that killed a horse by St Crued's Church. It stampeded across the bridge and into the Wool Shop – except then it was the Apothecary – the cat escaped into Crewdley Forest and was never seen again. That's why I don't like going into the Wool Shop sir. It gives me the creeps. I can see the Flacks on Trial in the Town Hall – the Judge was called Joseph John James Lacey ....."
"What did you say?"
"Joseph, John, James Lacey, Mr Mayor", Robespierre answered, stepping back from the bed and sneaking a look out of the window. It was raining.
"Lacey – you said Lacey – a Judge," the Mayor coughed, "what do you know about him?"
"He was a Judge sir – he sentenced the Flack sisters to be burned at the stake."
"Get out!" said the Mayor, "I've heard enough!"
"Yes sir – shall I wash the car?"
"Absolutely," the Mayor replied blankly, his mind on neither car nor chauffer. He repeated his affirmation as Robespierre left the room. "Absolutely, absolutely – my God," he murmured, "the Flack's ... witches ..... Lacey a Judge ..... a Scottish wild cat .... Sharon Hayes .... rolling around my carpet."
The vision of the Corpse on the Bridge returned. The Mayor shuddered. He needed to think – put it all in context. Robespierre, the Flacks – the usual idiocy - no – everything was just about normal.
"Robespierre!" he yelled. His man reappeared almost immediately.
"Yes sir!"
"Omelette and garlic mushrooms – hot tea! I'll be down in two minutes."
"Yes sir!" said Robespierre, "coming right up!
"No – I'm coming right down – sod off and cook!"
Robespierre beat it downstairs to the kitchen, cooked the omelette, made the tea and took it through to the Mayor's dining room. Crewdley's First Citizen was waiting at the table. Robespierre put the plate down and stepped back. The Mayor enjoyed the eggs and then the tea. He sat back in his chair.
"Robespierre ...."
"Yes sir?"
"Don't ever bring Sharon Hayes into this building again!"
"Certainly not Your Worship".

"Joseph, John, James Lacey."
"Yes Your Worship."
"You've been in the Reference Section at the Library!"
"No sir!"
"The internet then?"
"I can't use it sir."
"You found a very old history book under a loose floorboard in your room!"
"No sir."
"More tea", said the Mayor. Robespierre picked up the mug and was gone.
"He's lost the plot", he mumbled, "that young woman has scrambled his brain."

*

The Flacks were still knitting and Brittany was looking after the shop. "Four nil to Spain", said Myrtle. "So let's both knit little red football shirts for the teddy bears. We'll drop the blue ones."
"Of course – no one likes a loser," said Dorothy.
"But what about our Italian customers?" Myrtle asked, "do you think they will be offended?"
"I doubt it", Dorothy answered, "they've got bigger fish to fry than teddy bear's shirts."
"Well quite," agreed Myrtle, "international trade has to go on."
And so the sisters continued to knit, Claws stretched out on the carpet and Brittany served several young men who seemed captivated by angora, mohair and various shades of Shetland wool. Capitalism was not all about Banking scams – the London Interbank Offered Rate of Interest (Libor). No – the Flack's would pursue their own brand of commerce, much related to Wool and Cotton Socks (WACS)

*

The Mayor walked into the Town Clerk's office. "Beard!" he snapped, "you're a bit of a local history observer – is that right?"
Beard stopped writing up the minutes of the Planning and Highways committee. "Yes Your Worship. I think it's vital we know where we came from and what happened in our town. It does rather help to put things into perspective."
"Quite! Well find out all you can about a Crewdley family called Lacey – and while you're at it – check out the Flacks - the Civil War period seems a good time to start. You do use the internet don't you?"
"Yes sir! I knew it would come in useful for you one day."
"Maybe," the Mayor told him, "but until I tell you otherwise – keep sending the Council Agendas out by post – I insist! The prospect of Crewdley Councillors posting blogs and sending emails is not imminent, feasible or sensible."
"No sir – snail mail it is!"
The Mayor stared at the Town Clerk, "Lacey and the Flacks – priority!"
"Yes sir – I shall present you with a hard copy."
The Mayor continued to stare, "Just do it Beard, and bring it to me personally – none of your internal post or putting it in a pile of papers marked, 'Council Communications'. As soon as you've finished – tell me - morning , noon, or night."
"Yes sir – Lacey and the Flacks – Civil War and after," said Beard quietly.

The Mayor turned and went out of the Town Clerks small office, the walls of which were decorated with extremely boring pictures of heavy machinery laying tarmac, various tables and information extolling the virtues of local tourist spots, the forestry industry, places of worship, the health centre at Doctor Scargreaves Practice, community policing, a vets, a local football team, a women's hockey team, first aid procedures, fire regulations, contacts for a male voice choir, a gym, a women's hairdressers and - a map of Crewdley Town Centre. What more could a Town Clerk want?

*

Edwin Grimley was sitting upright in his best and biggest limousine at the head of a funeral courtage. The church service had been uneventful, and now the recently deceased would be laid to rest in the cemetery with all the dignity afforded by Crewdley's most eminent (and only) funeral service operator! It was raining heavily, a few people scuttled about the street as the cars pulled away from St Creud's Church.
"Mind that cat in the gutter by Flack's Wool Shop," Grimley instructed his driver, "it seems to be chasing a mouse or a rat."
"That's Claws," the driver answered, "I wouldn't want to run him over. The Flacks would never forgive me."
He drove slowly past the Wool Shop. Grimley looked across the road to his left. "Typical!" he said gruffly, "some people have no respect for funerals. Look at that!"
The driver glanced across where Grimley was sitting. Percy Fish was taking Pongo for a walk on a lead.
"That pig has got a banana in its mouth," said Grimley, "I'm sure there's a by-law against that sort of thing."
"Probably," agreed the driver, "the trouble is the pig can't read."

*

"Interesting – very interesting," said Beard as he scrolled down the computer page of the historical information relating to Crewdley and its former citizens. "My word! It's a wonder the town wasn't burnt to the ground."

*

As the funeral cortege went slowly over Crewdley Bridge, Grimley spied Willie Wottle and Derek Daub carrying buckets and ladders without enthusiasm or any protection from the rain.
"A window cleaners life is not a happy one," said Grimley.
"Times are tough," the driver agreed, "but they're not unemployed so they don't claim benefits. At least they've got their dignity."
Grimley looked at them from the comfort and dryness of his limo.
"Do you think so?" he asked.
"They're proud men," the driver insisted.
"So were their great grand fathers and they ended up in the work house," added Grimley, "keep the speed down. I don't want a ticket!"
"Most unlikely," the driver told him, "the local cop is on holiday."
"Typical," said Grimley, "it's a good job Crewdley is a law abiding town. But he might as well have put an advert in the 'Weekly Weaver' - I'm going on holiday, so all you burglars and petty criminals, make sure you get in and out before I get back! "In a small town like this, everybody will know he's in Spain by tonight."
"Malta actually," the driver told him.

"It makes no difference," Grimley insisted, "the fact remains that we shall have no police in the town for the next two weeks."
"One week," said the driver, "he's got to come back by next Friday. He's doing a session on ensuring your property is securely fixed when you leave home. You know – making sure you lock all the doors and close the windows – that sort of thing."
"How interesting," said Grimly, "he needs to put his own house in order first. I was walking past the Police Station earlier and the office door was wide open."
"Oh dear – do you think the Police Station has been burgled?" the driver asked.
"I doubt it," said Grimley, "there's absolutely nothing of any value in there."

*

Wottle and Daub presented themselves, with ladders and buckets, into the foyer of Crewdley Town Hall. They were soaked and dripping water poured off them as if they were standing in a shower.
"I saw you come in," said Beard, "I suppose you've come to clean the windows?"
"Is that a trick question?" asked Wottle.
"No," said Beard, "you'd better get on with it."
"I need to use your tap," said Daub.
"Carry on," Beard told him, "I shall be in my office if you need me."
"You can hold the ladder if you like," Wottle replied, "then Derek can go and put a bet on the two o' clock race at Ludlow."
"I've got no cash," Daub responded, "do you fancy having a little bet with us Mr Beard? You put the money up and we give you a cast-iron guarantee tip straight from the horse's mouth. I know one of the jockeys – Water Wheel – it's bound to win in this weather, ain't it?"
Beard looked at the men – unkempt, soaking wet, down at heel. They did not appear to have caused Ronnie Bettinger, the Crewdley bookmaker, any financial problems thus far.
"No thanks," Beard told them, "and if it carries on raining like this, the only horses that will be racing at Ludlow today will be sea horses. But please don't let me stop you from making a monetary contribution to Bettingers welfare fund – good morning gentlemen." Beard walked off, leaving Wottle and Daub slightly confused.
"Sea horses," said Willie Wottle.
"Welfare fund," said Derek Daub, "what's he on about?"
"I thought he was supposed to be intelligent," added Wottle, "he obviously knows nothing about horse racing."
"Nor window cleaning," said Daub, "and that tip I gave him - I think he just looked a gift horse in the mouth – which you shouldn't do – and he refused it!"
"Some people," said Wottle, "let's get on with it Derek before it gets dark."

*

That nights meeting of Crewdley Town Council was uneventful – a preliminary discussion about the Christmas Lights, a small donation to a Charity, an update on Parks and Gardens, and a report that skate-boarders were using the car park as a sports event venue.
"So call the police," said one Councillor.
"He's on holiday," said another.
"Next item," the Mayor said without enthusiasm. He was deep in thought about the Lacey Monument and the Witch Trials of Crewdley – if they ever took place.

"Any other business?" he asked, "No? Good! Next meeting - August 3rd – goodnight!"
Robespierre picked up the Mace, and the Mayor followed him out of the Council Chamber. They retired to the Mayor's Parlour and Robespierre set the Mace on its stand.
"Crewdley Blanc!" said the Mayor, "and get one for yourself – and lock the door. I don't want Councillors wandering in here. It gives them ideas above their status. Is it still raining Robespierre?"
Robespierre looked through the window. "Yes sir," he said, "cats and dogs."
Robespierre poured the drinks. "Racing was cancelled today," he said, "and I had a hot tip – Water Wheel in the 2 o'clock."
"Who gave you that tip?" the Mayor asked.
"The Town Clerk sir," he replied.
"And where did he get that unimpeachable information?" the Mayor asked him.
"A jockey," said Robespierre.
"Rubbish! Beard doesn't know any jockeys!"
"Well," Robespierre said slowly, "it wasn't a direct tip – more of a second hand one."
"Meaning what exactly."
"Someone in the pub, I expect."
"Have the window cleaners been today Robespierre?"
"Yes Mr Mayor."
"That's it then! The hot tip was from Messrs Wottle and Daub – two of Crewdley's biggest losers. Don't ever bet Robespierre – it's a mugs game."
"No sir," said Robespierre, "another drink sir?"
The Mayor held out his glass and Robespierre filled it with white wine.
"May I take it that I have been forgiven Your Worship?" Robespierre asked.
"Possibly," said the Mayor, "but never forgotten."
The bottle was soon empty and another opened. The rain continued to fall and the drink continued to flow until well into the night. At just after one a.m., the Mayor turned to Robespierre and said, "There's a black cat asleep on my chair -where did it come from – who let it in?"
Robespierre looked aghast, "It's the Flack's cat Claws."
"Take it out!" said the Mayor, "put it on the stairs outside."
"I don't like it," Robespierre spluttered, "I think it's the Civil war cat – the one that killed the horse."
The Mayor picked the cat up, opened the door and put it onto the landing. "Black coffee," he said sharply, and brush the seat of my chair. I don't want cat hairs all over my trousers."
Robespierre smiled as he remembered his and Sharon's unexpected entry into the Parlour. "No sir," he agreed, "we should always look our best, particularly in the Parlour. We shouldn't have cat hair on our trousers, nor lipstick or powder."
The Mayor knocked back the wine in his glass, "Black coffee," he said, "and don't be impertinent!"

*

Chapter 3

Bernard Beard knocked the door of the Mayor's Parlour and waited for a response. "Enter!" yelled a voice, and he did.

"Mr Mayor, "he said firmly, "I've got the information on the Flacks and Laceys."

"Sit down," said the Mayor, "and give me the papers."

The Town Clerk handed them over and sat back as the Mayor began to read.

"Joseph Lacey, Bewdley Town Clerk 1802 – 1896, son of James and Elizabeth, plantation owners of Jamaica, Justice of the Peace. The Lacey family were slave owners in Jamaica. Joseph Lacey – first of the recorded family tree – went to Jamaica on the orders of Oliver Cromwell to seize the island from the Spanish in 1655, under Admirals Pennard and Venables. Lacey was awarded a large Plantation that was worked by negroe slaves taken from Africa through the Port of London to Virginia and then to the Caribbean island of Jamaica."

The Mayor breathed in deeply and continued ......"Lacey imported indentured peasant labourers from England, Ireland, Scotland and Wales. Lacey became a wealthy man and established a family dynasty in the Falmouth area in the Jamaican county of Cornwall. Lacey and his wife of African descent had twelve children. He died around 1700. The family remained in Jamaica though some descendents returned to England."

"Very interesting," the Mayor said, "Lacey was a slave owner."

"Yes sir," said Beard, "one of his clan became Crewdley Town Clerk – just before my own family inherited the position."

"I suppose he ran on the anti-slavery ticket," the Mayor quipped.

"Slavery was banned 80 years before my grandparent became Town Clerk."

"But he would therefore have known all about Lacey," suggested the Mayor, "like I told you Beard, he ran on an anti-slavery ticket."

"Perhaps so Mr Mayor," Beard answered.

"You've got a liberal in the family – I'm surprised you never put yourself up for election."

"Far too risky," he answered quickly, "I prefer the solid routine of my office to the trap-door of local politics."

The Mayor looked at him with disdain and continued to read the papers, but was rudely interrupted by Beard.

"I have a confession Your Worship – my great, great, great great, great grandfather was 56 when he inherited the position of Town Clerk."

"So what?" the Mayor said curtly.

"Hardly a young man going into local government for a career, is it Mr Mayor?"

"A tradition upheld by you," the Mayor declared.

"Yes sir," Beard agreed, "but at least I shall get a decent pension."

"Assuming the Government doesn't bankrupt the country first," said the Mayor, "now zip it Beard and let me read about the Flacks!"

"The Flack Family has been established in Crewdley since Medieval times, Oh God!," the Mayor groaned, "the Flacks have been around since the blasted town was put up!"

"Yes sir," agreed Beard, "and it gets worse."

The Mayor read on .... "The Flacks have always kept that surname, whether male or female. In 1605 a male forbear was associated with the Gunpowder Plot, but fled to France before he could be arrested. In 1087 Peter Flack was mentioned in the Domesday Book as being a serf owned by Baron Crewdley. In 1494, John Flack was hung for stealing a turnip form Baron Crewdley. In 1639, Dorothy and Myrtle Flack were registered as living at number 6 Grubbers Alley – "Typical!" said the Mayor before continuing to read. "During the Crewdley Witch Trials of 1642, the Flack sisters were tried for Witchcraft by Justice John Lacey. The women were put in a ducking stool in Crewdley pond (since filled in) and they floated. The guilty verdict decreed by Justice Lacey was a formality. They were accused of flying at night on broomsticks around St Crued's Church and causing a wild cat to kill a horse.

Their many children cursed the Lacey family for eternity and in 1645, John Lacey was found dead in a cider press in the cottage garden on the edge of Crewdley Forest. His body had been crushed to a pulp by the apple stone which weighed in excess of one ton.

After the Judges death, the Lacey family left Crewdley for the New World. Various family members returned to the Crewdley area around 1820."

The Mayor put the papers on the table. "I don't know any Laceys," he said coldly, "unfortunately the Flacks are still with us."

"There are two Lacey's on the electoral register, Your Worship – just on the edge of Crewdley Forest - Cider Cottage I think it's called."

*

The Mayor looked through the window of the Rolls Royce into Crewdley Forest. "About another half a mile then pull in near Cider Cottage. I just want to look the place over."

"Yes sir," said Robespierre, "will go".

"If I wanted an American chauffer Robespierre I would advertise for one – English!"

Robespierre drove smoothly along the winding road until he saw the cottage. He did as he was told, parked up and turned the engine off.

"It's all very green," he said to the Mayor, "all that rain Your Worship. If it was warmer we could grow rice. As it is, I expect water buffalo will be used to plough the fields any day now."

"Shut up," the Mayor told him.

"Sir!"

The Mayor could see the cottage through the trees and there in the garden, almost hidden by brambles, was a huge round stone.

"It's the cider press!" he said sharply, "it's still there after nearly 400 years!"

*

"It's Mr Salvatori," Myrtle told Dorothy, "would you like to speak to him?"

Dorothy nodded and Myrtle passed the phone.

"Good afternoon Mr Salvatori .... very well thank you ...... yes .... a lot of rain ......oh that's nice .....ninety degrees in Scicily .... yes .... wonderful .....please go ahead – we are ready to trade - thank you – and please give our very best wishes to Mr Luigi - bye bye."

"How nice to be doing business again with our Italian partners," said Myrtle.

"I didn't mention the football result," said Dorothy.

"Best not," agreed Myrtle, "perhaps they will do better at the Olympics?"

*

One of the shops between the bank and the Mayor's Parlour had been empty for some weeks. The "For Rent" sign had already been splattered by seagulls and pigeon mess, and the birds had taken to using it as a convenient perch. But on Monday 9th July, the sign was taken down by flunkeys of Messrs Dilettante and Doppler, the Crewdley Estate Agents and Auctioneers. The flunkey's were Wottle and Daub, grateful for the work, and always available to risk life and limb by stepping up a ladder, past its best, positioned on the uneven paving stones of Church Street, hanging off an old building to earn an honest couple of quid.
The Mayor, of course, noticed this activity. A new business always caused him a certain degree of apprehension - until it had settled down and become part of Crewdley's commercial life. The recent record of new ventures was not good. They came and went in rapid succession – shops selling party novelties and cards, flower shops, a discount shop, clothes shops etc. Charity shops were now very firmly established, as were one or two new restaurants. What next?

*

On Tuesday 10th, the Mayor noticed shop fitters going about their business. He also noticed lorries with Italian registration plates coming over the bridge and going up towards the Forest. Curiosity caused him to instruct Robespierre to be ready with the Rolls Royce. They drove out of town and up into Crewdley Forest. There was no mistaking the lorries destination – Cider Cottage.

"Pull over!" said the Mayor," and stop the car."
Robespierre did as he was told. They saw the lorry being unloaded by two men who took the boxes into sheds near the cottage.
"Mafia," Robespierre said quietly.
"Maybe," the Mayor answered, "we've seen enough for now – let's go Robespierre."
They stopped for a drink at "The Forest Hotel" – the Mayor had wine and Robespierre a lemonade. The Mayor had two more – Robespierre did not.
"Something is going on," the Mayor declared to the lemonade drinker, "and I don't like it one little bit!"

*

The Shop Fitters worked all day and night and the grand opening took place on Wednesday 11th. It was a Fruit and Vegetable Emporium – apples, grapes, oranges, lemons, fennel, asparagus, figs, tomatoes, lettuces – and outside in designer Italian jugs, was an attractive display of summer flowers, ferns and small exotic plants.
The Mayor stood on the pavement outside and looked at the name over the shop window – "Flacks, Flowers, Fruit and Vegetables,"
"I knew it!" the Mayor said to Robespierre, "the Italian mob are using them as a front!"
He instructed Robespierre to take him back to Cider Cottage.
They got out of the car and approached a man in the garden.
"Good morning Mr Mayor," he said, "welcome to Cider Cottage."
"You've got that cider press working," the Mayor said calmly.
"Indeed," the man said, "and my old donkey doesn't mind a few turns with the stone. He knows after ten minutes he'll get apples and a couple of sticks of fennel."
"You are being used as a front for the Mafia," the Mayor told him.
"Nonsense!" replied the man, "as you can see, I am pressing olives. I'm going to bottle them and the Flacks will sell them."
"Ah! There's the rub," said the Mayor, "the Flacks!"

"Two little innocent old ladies," the man said laughing, "they saw a gap in the market, that's all!"
"You are John Lacey," said the Mayor.
"So what?"
"Do you know your family history? Do you know the history of that stone press?"
"No I don't – except I do know that my family were charcoal burners in the Forest – peasants really – but honest folk for all that."
"And your relationship with the Flacks?"
"Simple! They knew about the cider press and asked if I could press their olives – come on here Billy – have an apple."
He gave the donkey an apple and followed it round the stone as it ate it.
"I've seen enough," the Mayor said, "come on Robespierre. Let's get back to town."

Lacey watched them go and patted the donkey as it walked round, pulling the large stone that crushed the olives, "City folk," he said, "good boy Billy – nearly finished."

*

And so Crewdley's newest business was open to the public. The Mayor was suspicious. The Flacks first few days of trading went very well. Brittany Baxter was put in charge – Myrtle and Dorothy preferred the quietness of the Wool Shop.

*

Bernard Beard gave the Mayor a simple sheet of paper.
"It's an update Mr Mayor," he said, "the Lacacy's were charcoal burners in the forest – peasants really."
"I know that," the Mayor told him, "find out if there's any connection between the Lacey's and Italy."
"There isn't," said Beard, "there's the Jamaican connection, but not Italian."
"What about the Flacks?"
"The Flack family took in Italian prisoners of war in 1945," Beard told him, "they had been working around Crewdley in the fields. Two of them stayed until 1950 – a Mr Salvatori and a Mr Luigi."
"That's it!" said the Mayor, "pay back time!"

*

Chapter 4

The London Olympics came and went. Crewdley continued its reputation as a backwater of civic, political and economic life. However, events had moved on a fraction with reference to the local economy. The Flacks Wool Shop was still benefitting from the shining effect of Brittany Baxter. And here's the rub - the girl was multi-tasking! The Flacks had encouraged her to spend time at the Fruit and Veg Emporium as a sort of mobile manageress. They increased her wages and took on two other young women to help out. But it was Brittany who dazzled amongst the plums and peaches and sizzled between the satumas and celery. Trade was brisk. In fact, it was hard to imagine how the citizens of Crewdley had managed before Flacks Fruit and Veg had opened. The most interesting fact about the new venture was definitely that the Flacks had introduced the citizens to the delights of exotic fruits and vegetables. There was one item in particular that had established itself as the new favourite on the palate of Crewdley folk .

Olives! Who would have believed it? The best Sicilian olives sold like hot cakes, if that is not too peculiary inept an analogy?

Never was it envisaged by anyone that olives could become an integral part of the Crewdley diet. Even Percy Fish was converted to this part of the new epicurean diet. And so was Pongo the Pig! He loved the olives, and Percy bought them by the kilo. And olive oil was a real best seller. As long as it had the magic words on the label of the elegant bottles – "Luigi and Salvatori Best Sicilian Olive oil – pressed and bottled in Crewdley".

The Mayor was not happy. It was true that the Italians had not actually threatened him with being garrotted or thrown off the balcony of Crewdley Town Hall. But it was all too smooth, too matter of fact. One minute, a redundant novelty shop trying to sell revolting Tricks or Treats to children – imitation dog mess, false wounds and horrific skin injuries, phoney eyes that shot out on springs, and the good old favourite – Dracula's Teeth! Closure was inevitable. And suddenly, from nowhere, the Mafia and some anonymous non-voter from Crewdley Forest was operating a one ton ancient cider press for crushing olives.

The lorries from Sicily were regular over Cewdley Bridge on their way up to the Forest. That was after the drivers had declared a partial road closure outside the Fruit and Veg Emporium to deliver their produce. Each Tuesday was quite an event. For an hour or so the drivers unloaded and if it wasn't pouring with rain or freezing, they set up chairs and a table on the pavement and ate their lunch with Brittany.

Red wine was served, oblivious to the fact that the local cop usually hovered around out of interest, and even on occasion joined them at the table for a re-freshment – wine, bread, cheese, olives! The Flacks would join in. What a happy little congregation.

The Mayor was watching one such assembly from the Town Hall window. "Look at this Robespierre!" he said sternly, "it's virtually a street party".

"Perhaps the police should be called," Robespierre answered.

"Good idea," said the Mayor, "except that he's on his second glass of wine and looks all set to eat his way through his second bowl of olives."

*

John Lacey had adapted easily to pressing Sicilian olives instead of cider apples. Luigi and Salvatori paid him extremely well. He still pressed a few cider apples and did a little bottling of his 'Lacey's Cider' which he sold at the "Forest Hotel" and one or two local outlets, such as "The Star and Garter."

Since the Mayor's first encounter with Lacey, Robespierre had been inquisitive about 'Lacey's Cider' and had now taken to drinking it. A bottle had found its way into the Mayor's Parlour.
"Robespierre!" the Mayor yelled, "what is this!".
"A bottle of cider your worship," answered Robespierre.
"Where did you buy it?"
"From the 'Star and Garter,' your worship. "It's very good. Sharon swears by it."
"Yes, swears at it and gargles with it I expect."
Robespierre grinned. "She's a good girl."
"No she isn't!" the Mayor declared, "she is forbidden fruit."
"Funny you should say that Mr Mayor," added Robespierre, "Sharon has started working part time at Flack's Fruit and Veg."
"Good God!" the Mayor exclaimed, "is there no end to the Flacks web of intrigue? It will all end in tears. The Italian connection has not yet shown itself in its true colours."
"Sharon hasn't spotted anything peculiar," said Robespierre.
"She wouldn't! She sees life in a haze of vodka fumes. Her idea of peculiar is anybody drinking singles. Don't you dare confide any Council business to that young woman."
"She might stand for Council," said Robespierre. She was impressed by her time in this building."
"She was drunk," the Mayor said angrily, "and you said she thought she was in the betting shop."
"Did I? Robespierre enquired, "well anyway, Sharon has got plans for the future."
"Just as long as you are not part of those plans Robespierre. And if that young woman ever does decide to stand for Council, you bring her Nomination Papers to me, right?"

"Right!" said Robespierre. He paused then asked the question, "why Mr Mayor?"
"So that I can make sure the papers never get anywhere near Beard. She will not get the Mayoral stamp of approval while I'm around."
Another pause, then, "I didn't think that was required," Robespierre declared.
"It is," the Mayor said, "local Government Act, section two, paragraphs one to three."
"Oh," said Robespierre, "I didn't know that."

*

Saturday 3rd August 2013 was a warm day in Crewdley. In the appropriately named Gardeners Meadow, the Mayor spoke clearly into the microphone. "Good morning citizens of Crewdley, welcome everyone to our Annual Horticultural Show. I am sure that you will be delighted with the quality and range of products displayed here today, as indeed I have been myself. If there are any finer fruits, vegetables and flowers grown anywhere in the country, then let them compete with us directly, here in Crewdley. The judges are making their way around the displays. It won't be too long before we have our winners. And then the public will be able to purchase as much as the growers wish to sell. So enjoy the day. Support your local Charities and let us show our appreciation to the organisers of today's event in the usual way."
The Mayor handed the microphone to Robespierre and began to clap. Light applause echoed around the Meadow.
"Come on Robespierre," he said "it's time for our slow and dignified walk around the stalls. And keep one step behind me."
"Yes Mr Mayor"! said Robespierre, " I know my place and I'm proud to serve."
"Shut up!"
They began their slow walk to the stalls. A good day, an honest day. What could possibly go wrong?

The Mayor approached the first stall and went directly to the man standing behind it. "What on earth are you doing here Lacey?" he asked, "you are not fruit, flowers or vegetables."
"I'm Lacey's Cider," declared Lacey, "it's the wine, beer and cider section. Home brewing is very popular. Would you like to try a glass?"
"Yes please", said Robespierre.
"No thank you," the Mayor said firmly, "I need to keep a very clear mind."
He walked off with Robespierre in tow.
"That man is working his way into Crewdley society" he said tersely, "Don't trust him."
"He only sells cider Your Worship," Replied Robespierre.
"Wrong again!" the Mayor said through gritted teeth as he walked on, "Lacey is the producer of Sicilian olive oil, as imported by Messer's Luigi and Salvatori, and sold to the Crewdley public by the Flack sisters. He's literally oiling the wheels of corruption."
"With his cider press sir?" asked Robespierre.
"Correct! And last week the Licensing Committee gave the Flacks permission to sell alcohol in their Emporium."
"Yes sir," said Robespierre, "Sharon is very pleased about that."
"I'll bet she is. So I suppose any day now "Lacey's Cider" will be on sale, with Brittany Baxter and Sharon Hayes appearing as Greek hand maidens, and offering glasses of cider and vodka to customers who go in for potatoes!"
"I think they go in to see Brittany and Sharon Mr Mayor. The samples of cider and vodka are icing on the cake. Also Mr Mayor and I know you like to be kept up to speed on these issues ..... Lacey is pressing and distilling potatoes to make vodka. He makes it, the Flacks sell it, customers drink it. It's a growing business, you could say Mr Mayor. They're all making money. Even Mr McGurk is in a bit of a temper about it all. The Flacks seem to be becoming the place to be seen at."
"Don't be so ridiculous!" the Mayor snapped, "and remember what I told you Robespierre. Keep that young woman out of the Town Hall."
"That's a big 10 – 4!" said Robespierre, stopping quickly to let the Mayor get a step ahead.
"Idiot!" said the Mayor, and then he noticed something that made his blood run cold.
The Flacks were positioned on chairs behind a fruit and vegetable stall. The Judges were inspecting the produce.
"Olives aren't local produce," the Mayor said to Robespierre, "and look at all that cabbage. They've probably got it from Tesco."
The Judges hovered, the Flacks smiled sweetly as the two men in Italian suits stood closely by watching procedures.
"That Luigi and Salvatori!" said the Mayor "They're intimidating the Judges!"
"I wouldn't get involved if I were you," suggested Robespierre, "it might not be appreciated."
The Mayor watched the scene like a hawk. The Italians were impassive, inscrutable and menacing. "Shall we walk on Your Worship?"
"Yes Robespeare," he answered, "I think you're right." And they did.
But the next stall was bizarre and the Mayor was dumbfounded. "Percy Fish!" he said loudly, "what are you doing here? And you've got that pig with you."
"Pongo!" said Percy, "Yes Mr Mayor. I am displaying truffles ... fruits of the forest. Pongo snouts 'em out and I collect them in a sack. Delicious fried in a pan with butter. There's also mushrooms, wild garlic, chives and a few wild gooseberries ... want some?"

"Give me three or four truffles in a brown paper bag. Robespierre .... take them!"
"That'll be thirty pounds for three," said Percy Fish.
"They had better be good," said the Mayor, paying Fish, "if I like them I might order more ..... and I'd like a discount."
"I'll see what I can do," Fish answered as he popped a truffle into Pongo's mouth.
"That pig has just eaten ten pounds of your money," said the Mayor.
"He's worth it," Fish replied, "bless his little cotton socks."
The Mayor looked hard at Fish and then at Robespierre. He walked away slowly and shook his head. "Why me?" he mumbled under his breath, "why me?"
The Mayor and his officer walked on. Many stalls were delightful with flowers that Chelsea would envy. Vegetable produce was prolific .... carrots, potatoes, cabbage, beetroot and many more. Other stalls displayed tempting fruits – plums, early apples, raspberries, strawberries, gooseberries ... all presented exquisitely and with pride.
The gardeners of Crewdley had excelled. There were stalls with hoop-la, coconut shys, lucky dips, tombola, even a donkey was there for the children to ride. A few small tents had been erected in which commercial items were offered for sale to the public – cheap radios, jewellery, clothing – just the kind of rubbish available at many High Street Markets.
The Mayor and Robespierre gravitated back to Flacks, but kept a respectable distance. The Judges were deep in conversation. The Italians were still there. And then, the Mayor noticed, each side of the huge cabbage display - nectarines, bananas, pineapples, kiwi fruits ...." Robespierre!" he said sharply, "look at that lot! If any of that is grown in Crewdley we'd all better start wearing Bermuda shorts and sandals! And look at that display of olives! It's outrageous!"
Robespierre gawped, "They do say climate change is with us Your Worship."
"Oh shut up you fool! This is a clear breach of regulations ... it's local produce only ... not imports from the Caribbean! No wonder the Judges are in a mess. Look at those Italians! They're putting the frighteners on them."
The Judges were indeed arguing in the polite way one would expect – firm, resolute statements, sharp intakes of breath, mutterings, exclamations – all delivered in the tones expected perhaps from a Librarian who has been given a returned book from a lender three months over the expiry date, but who doesn't really want to make him or her cough up a piddling fine.
Finally, one of the Judges placed a Winners Rosette onto the Flacks display. "Outrageous!" said the Mayor, The Flacks smiled in their spooky way and shook hands with several Judges. Another Judge walked off brusquely, declaring, "I resign."
"A man of principal," said the Mayor. "He's a well known gambler," said Robespierre. "Be quiet", instructed the Mayor, "he's making a point about this fix."
"He owes Ronnie Bettinger a thousand pounds," Robespierre said helpfully.
"Shut up!" the Mayor retorted.
The Flacks were revelling in their win. "It's a great day for our shop," said Myrtle, admiring the rosette.
"Oh yes," agreed Dorothy, "we could put it on Claw's collar."
"Too big," exclaimed Myrtle, "it might stop him catching mice."
"I never thought of that," conferred Dorothy, "and thank you again," she called after the Judges as they shuffled away.
"I've seen enough Robespierre," the Mayor said, "bring the car round, it's time to go."

And so they retreated back to the Mayor's Parlour and the Mayor watched sport on television. Robespierre prepared the truffles in a pan with fried eggs. "Get the Crewdley Blanc!" the Mayor called, "and I'll have a Cuban cigar."

They ate and drank and smoked for an hour. "Ok", said the Mayor, "now get lost. I'm going round to Pippa Monroe's and I don't won't to be disturbed. And remember what I said about Sharon Hayes. She is not to come anywhere near this building."

"Absolutely!" said Robespierre.

The Mayor eyed his man as he left the Parlour. Robespierre looked back and stood to attention. "Clear up this mess and keep the door locked Robespierre."

"Yes sir!"

The Mayor went quickly down the elegant staircase and into the street. He let himself into Mrs Munroe's house with his key and went up to the first floor. "Pippa darling," he said enthusiastically as they kissed.

"Hello Harold," she responded warmly, "come and look at this!"

They walked to the window which provided the perfect view of the River Crewd and the bridge. "Isn't that Rupert Beard rowing a coracle?"

"Oh my God," the Mayor moaned, "who let him out in the daylight hours?"

*

Robespierre put another glass of vodka into Sharon's delicate hand. "Got any olives?" she enquired, knocking back the drink.

"I daren't bring them up here," replied the old boy from the Bastille. "The Mayor is not keen."

"Well I am," she insisted, "I'll have another vodka .... got any nuts?"

Robespierre got the nuts, put them into a dish and offered them to Sharon. "I like it in here," she declared, "so this is his Parlour, eh? I've got a feeling I've been in here before."

"Really," asked Robespierre, "I wouldn't know. We can't stay too long."

"Why not?"

"The Mayor might come back early."

"Sod him!" Sharon declared, knocking back her second vodka,

"Have some nuts," he suggested.

"Ta," she answered, "and I'll have another vodka."

And so it went on into the evening. Robespierre was very anxious. "I think it's time to go," he finally suggested, "we'll go out the back way, to avoid the Mayor."

He collected Sharon from the settee and helped her to the door. "I know you," she said unsteadily, "you're Robespierre aren't you?"

"I am," he answered, "quickly now Sharon. Hold onto me."

They negotiated the stairs carefully until they got out into the street. The Mayor was approaching towards them from the Bridge.

"Just carry on walking with me," Robespierre implored her, "and don't speak to him."

The Mayor walked up to Robespierre and looked him in the eye. "What are you doing with that young woman?"

"We've been to the 'Star and Garter' Your Worship. I'm taking Sharon home."

"Who is he?" she said loudly, "tell him we don't want any. Is he selling the Big Issue!"

"Come on Sharon, it's time to go."

"Ta –ra Granddad, " she called out loudly, get some olives in next time!"

*

Chapter 5

"It's true Your Worship," Robespierre said, "several of the Flower Show Judges have gone to Sicily on holiday. Sharon told me. The Flacks have gone as well. Brittany is in charge of the Flower Shop."
"It's happening," said the Mayor, "they're taking over. Get me Mrs Croker on the phone."
"Mrs Croker?" enquired Robespierre with real trepidation, "errm ..... I'd rather not Your Worship."
"Do it!" snapped the Mayor, "and I don't care if she does recognise you as the Lonely Hearts Club heavy breather. She's the only person in this town with a brain."
Robespierre rang for Mrs Croker at the Mercian Bank. "Hello" she answered, "who is this?"
"Robespierre ... the Mayor's Officer," replied, Anton the Reluctant.
"Look!" she snapped, "I'm not interested!"
"The Mayor wants a word," he said, "I'll put him on."
He passed the phone to Crewdley's finest.
"Good morning Mrs Croker," he said, "I would like to speak to you on a very serious issue."
"So go ahead," she suggested, "I'm busy."
"Not on the phone," he asserted, "how about lunch? I could pick you up at one o' clock and we could eat at The Forest Hotel."
A pause. The Mayor looked at Robespierre. Robespierre smiled his supercilious grin.
"Yes all right," she agreed, "I need to be back here within the hour. This bank doesn't run itself. You wouldn't believe the mess that Roland Jones left it in ... the bastard!"
"Ah!" said the Mayor, "the wound has still not healed. Yes of course I remember very well – one o' clock then .... bye."
He gave the phone back to Robespierre. "She's got a very good clear and incisive mind," said the Mayor, "I hope to God she never gets on the Council."
"Formidable", Robespierre exclaimed with a heavy French intonation.
"Robespierre," said the Mayor, "when will you ever rid yourself of your Frenchness?"
"Never!" he declared firmly, "it's in my blood Your Worship, my DNA. My veins run with the blood of la Belle France."
"You're English!" Presbyterian accused, "who do you cheer for when they play each other at Rugby?"
"France!" said Robespierre.
"Football?"
"France!"
"Cricket?"
"Ermm ....."
"Go and get the car out - wash it down and clean it. Be outside the Mercian Bank at one o'clock."
"What about my lunch Mr Mayor?" he asked pathetically.
"Typical peasant", said the Mayor, "always thinking of your stomach."
"But you'll be having a three course meal at "The Forest Hotel."

"Correct! And you'll be having a sandwich – if you're lucky. Sit in the car well away from me when you're eating your cheese and onion. I don't want you interfering. You are a distraction Robespierre. So keep out of my way until quarter to two."

"Yes sir," Robespierre conceded. "I might do a bit of bird watching when I'm waiting."
"Just don't get climbing any trees. That uniform costs money."
"I could do with a new one."
"So could I ....a new dog's body. Behave yourself."
Robespierre disappeared to wash the car. The Mayor looked out across the street to the bank. "The French don't even play cricket – idiot!"

*

The dining room of the "Forest Hotel" was quiet. The Mayor and Mrs Croker were the only customers. They had decided to have fish and a bottle of Crewdley Blanc.
"Have you got the banking business back into good order at the Mercian?" he asked her.
"Just about," she replied, sipping the wine, "we were a basket case. Expenditure was disastrously high – loans unpaid, outgoings at an unsustainable level, virtually no income or deposits – well one such person actually – that bastard Roland Jones – the so called manager."
"Ah yes," said the Mayor between mouthfuls of fish and potatoes, "he let the team down very badly."
"He absconded!" she declared, "said he was going to Portugal – probably with a young tart!" She drank more wine and helped herself to another glass from the bottle in the ice bucket.
"You were compromised," said the Mayor, "emotionally attached."
"Quite!" she snapped, "the pig!"
"A stalwart of the community and he blew it," the Mayor said helpfully.
"He didn't have a head for economics. He let pleasures of the flesh distract him."
The Mayor pondered this comment and drank more wine. "But if those pleasures of the flesh would have remained directed towards you, then things would have been tickety – boo."
"Quite .... the pig!" she said again.
The Mayor looked at Mrs Croker – a widow, good looking aged about forty, as smart as a skin burn. Yes ..... mmm ... she ... mmm well, he thought, no I mustn't let the carnal instincts take over, this is strictly a business meeting, a necessary arrangement made in an attempt to tackle the problem of the hour – the Flacks and their Italian cohorts.
"Noticed anything peculiar about Crewdley lately?" he asked her.
"Deposit accounts are coming back up," she said with a rather bored tone, "I'm giving out a few more loans and one or two mortgages."
"And?" the Mayor asked in expectation.
"And yes, there has been a noticeable change in the balance of the local economy."
"Yes?" the Mayor encouraged her, "where to?"
"The Flacks," she answered, "their Fruit, Veg and Flowers seem to be out-selling everybody.
And of course the olive oil and the vodka. Their revenue has gone through the roof. Their business and deposit account – She stopped short. "I'm saying too much. I'm in danger of disclosing a confidential business arrangement. Every customer deserves confidentiality. And they have their new partners, their new business associates – the Italians."
"Waiter!" the Mayor called, "more wine." It was duly delivered into the ice bucket. The Mayor poured the drinks and they both drank in polite sips. Another each. They drank faster, almost slurping. More fish, more wine, more talk.
"Waiter! Another bottle." The Mayor boomed.
It's two o'clock!" Mrs Croker exclaimed loudly, "I'm late for work!"

The Mayor put his hand on hers. “We are onto something important,” he told her, “work can wait – just this once, eh Mrs Croker?”
She was beginning to warm towards him – unrequited passion was being signalled that the wait could almost be over.
“Waiter!”
“Yes sir?” he said, appearing from nowhere.
“We have booked a room here for a private business meeting. Will you please take us up to it?”
The waiter looked confused, “Oh I didn’t realise”, he said, “certainly sir.”
And with that, the couple were shown up to a room, with the wine and glasses.
The door was closed behind them.
“Oh Harold,” she purred, putting her arms around his neck, “I think I am going to be able to help you in ever so many ways.”
They kissed with, at first respectful if guarded passion. But then inhibitions were dispensed with, “Mrs Croker,” he said, “I am truly delighted.”

*

Robespierre looked at his watch. It was two thirty. “He’s very late,” he mumbled, and then re-read an article in the “Daily Mirror”. He put the newspaper down and looked across the car park to the “Forest Hotel,” and then onto the front passenger seat. His cheese sandwiches did not look appealing, but he was hungry so he began to eat them. He swigged from a bottle of lemonade, “A civic lunch for him, and I get this!”
He took out a jar of pickles form the dashboard cubby-hole, got the lid off, scooped out a pickle, and crunched it. “Mmmm....good!”
He took another, but it slid from his fingers onto the floor, “Sod it,” he cursed and lent over to pick it up. He spilt the jar, pickles shot onto the passenger seat and half the jar of vinegar. “Oh dear,” he said, sitting back up with a start. He thought for a minute and then got out an air freshener. He sprayed the seat violently. It stank worse, so he opened his door and got out. “Sod it”, he said again, “he’s bound to notice,”
He retrieved the pickle jar, the sandwich papers and the lemonade bottle. He walked over to a litter bin and dropped his rubbish in.
He stood looking at the car. He took a cigar out of his top pocket and lit it. He walked slowly round the car park, smoking as he went. No sign of the Mayor and Mrs Croker, so he got back into the car and waited. The smell was overpowering, terrible and it took his breath away, making him wheeze and cough. So he put all the windows down and got back out, and facing the litter bin said, with some emotion,” The English are a pain in the arse!”

*

At six o’clock the Mayor and Mrs Croker came out of the hotel, each the worse for an afternoons drinking and debauchery. They got into the back seats of the car. “What’s that smell Robespierre?” he asked, “don’t tell me! Pickles and vinegar.”
“And hairspray,” added Mrs Croker, “my God are you trying to poison us?”
“It’s air freshener,” admitted Robespierre, “I apologise Mr Mayor.”
“Don’t bother,” he said through the haze which now engulfed them all, “just take Mrs Croker to the bank.”
“It’s closed now,” she said, “take me into Crewdley anyway and put me down by the church. I’ll walk home from there. I need a brisk walk to clear my head.”

"Will do," smirked Robespierre, "and yourself Mr Mayor – where to?"
"Home of course," the Mayor answered. "What's the matter with you? Have the fumes got to your brain? Of course home – as usual. Then park the car up and come to the Parlour. I've got a job for you."
"Yes sir," complied Robespierre as he drove the car away from the hotel. They passed the forest and Lacey's cottage.
"There it is," the Mayor pointed out, "the cider press and look ..... there's Lacey's donkey."
"Billy," said Robespierre helpfully.
"Shut up!"
"Sorry," said Robespierre.
"That's the new centre of economic activity. That's where he presses the olives and distils the vodka – from potatoes!" the Mayor scoffed.
The car travelled on towards Crewdley, through the forest and down into the town. Robespierre got out and opened the door for Mrs Croker.
"Bye," she said smiling to the Mayor.
"Bye," he answered her, "I'll be in touch."
Robespierre closed the door, got back in and drove behind the Town Hall. He opened the back door and the Mayor got out. Robespierre smiled knowingly.
"Shut up!" the Mayor said again. "It's nothing to do with you."

*

A few days later the Mayor was looking out of the Parlour window down into the street. Two men were hovering on the pavement opposite.
"Robespierre," he summoned his man, "you spend a lot of time hanging around in the street – who are those two?"
"Buskers," Robespierre replied.
"Unlicensed beggars," the Mayor affirmed, drinking wine from a civic glass, "get me some olives," he asked, "and I don't mean Flack's Italian ."
Robespierre went to the fridge and opened the door, "Greek ok?" he enquired.
"Yes. And I'll have a plate Of cheese - Cheshire - and I fancy a gherkin - oh yes – and go out and get some fresh brown bread. The money is in the syrup tin on the shelf."
Robespierre put the cheese and olives on a plate – "Polish gherkins ok?"
"Obviously," the Mayor replied, "but I refuse to give any of our money to the Flacks or Luigi and Salvatore."

Robespierre gave him the plate, "I'll go and get the bread."
"Good! Don't be long – I'm peckish."
Robespierre vacated the building and went to the bread shop where he purchased a French loaf. On his way back to the Parlour he walked past the buskers. One man was tapping a tambourine and the other strumming a small washboard. Their singing was an appalling row. A bucket was positioned at their feet. Robespierre looked in. It was empty. He walked on, crossed the street and went back up into the Mayor's Parlour. He cut the bread, put it onto another plate and gave it to the Mayor.
"Have a drink," said the Mayor, "get yourself a glass."
"Thank you sir," said Robespierre pouring a glass, "The buskers are terrible," he told him, "the worst I have ever heard. No money in their bucket."

"They're still begging. The fact that they have earned no money is a technicality," said the Mayor.
Bernard Beard knocked the door, and came in at the Mayor's call.
"Agenda item for the Licensing Committee," he said, "Busking!"
"Yes your worship," Beard responded, "it's quite a racket. Actually, I can hear it from my office if the window is open and the wind is blowing North to South. It's the same as crows. They get in the chimneys. Seagulls now as well….."
"Beard!" the Mayor shouted, "just make sure Busking is an Agenda item."
The little man stood to attention, "Yes sir – sorry sir."
With that, he scooted from the Parlour back to his broom cupboard of an office. It doesn't pay to cross the Mayor – memory like an elephant's and vindictive.
"Idiot!" said the Mayor.
"Absolutely!" agreed Robespierre, "he's hopeless."
"I meant you," the Mayor told him, "this cheese is Lancashire – I said Cheshire. Get it right!"
"Sorry," apologised Robespierre, "how is the gherkin?"

*

The Buskers were at it again outside the Mayors' Parlour. "I'm getting annoyed with those two clowns," the Mayor said to Robespierre, "go down and bring them in here to me."
Robespierre hovered, rocked back on his heels and pondered the instruction.
"Do you want them to play for you Mr Mayor?"
The Mayor looked hard at his chauffer cum valet dogsbody. Robespierre continued to move on and off his toes. He smirked, then frowned and scratched his nose.
"Play for me? Do you really think that I want those two idiots to perform for me?"
"Not sure sir."
"They've got no shame and no talent. Their performance is the next thing to being put in the stocks. Public humiliation is what they are all about. Go out and bring them to me."
Robespierre turned on his heels and made his exit. The Mayor went to the window and looked down to the street. Robespierre approached the men. They stopped using the tambourine and washboard and looked up to the window.
"My God," the Mayor mumbled, "those idiots." A minute or two later, the Parlour door was knocked.
"Enter!" boomed the Mayor. They did.
"Wattle and Daub!" The Mayor shouted, "What the hell do you think you are doing?"
"Playing music, " said Wottle.
"Singing," said Daub.
"Don't be absurd! You two have absolutely no musical talent whatsoever."
"We were interviewed for "The Voice" on the BBC," said Wottle.
"What happened?" the Mayor asked.
"They said no," answered Daub, "but we left our card."
"You're living in a dream world," the Mayor told them, "you can't even clean windows without dropping the bucket. You're both a disaster waiting to happen."
"Ah!" said Wottle as if he had solved an eternal question known only to the Gods, "that's why we changed our profession."
"Profession!" scoffed the Mayor, "hardly that, eh boys? Where are your qualifications?"
"We left school early," Daub explained, "had to earn a living."

"But you didn't, did you?" You scoot around Crewdley doing odd jobs – window cleaning was your latest wheeze – and now this."
He paused and looked them up and down. "You realise it's illegal to beg don't you?"
"We don't beg," answered Wottle, "we perform."
"It's illegal!" the Mayor declared, "you didn't apply to this office or anywhere else."
"We're not very good at paperwork," Daub declared, "so we just thought we'd give it a go."
The Mayor looked hard at the pathetic pair. "How much have you earned with that washboard and tambourine?"
"Forty three pence Mr Mayor," said Wottle.
"And for how long have you been inflicting grief onto the citizens of Crewdley – how long have you been performing?"
"About three weeks," Daub declared in a tone which combined hopeless resignation with just a hint of pathetic spirit.
"Just a little over fourteen pence a week," the Mayor confirmed, "first the good news – you could possibly claim a tax rebate for your equipment depreciating over the many years you might expect to be performing your act before you have earned enough to retire."
"We don't pay income tax," they said together.
"No," said the Mayor, "it was a rhetorical statement – I knew the answer. Which leads me nicely on to the bad news....."
"What's that?" Wottle enquired.
"We don't have a Workhouse anymore, " the Mayor declared. Wottle and Daub looked blank.
"Workhouse?" said Daub, "we rent in Dark Lane."
"How very appropriate. Who pays your rent?"
"We get Housing Benefit," said Wottle with just a hint of arrogance, "and a Council tax rebate."
"And Job seekers Allowance, free prescriptions, free eye tests and free dental treatment," Daub added, "we didn't qualify for Winter Fuel Allowance or free bus passes."
"It's just a matter of time lads," the Mayor added, "hang on in there. It comes to he who waits. But tell me, how do you see your careers panning out until then? The London Palladium? A giant car washing demonstration at the O2 Arena? A sponsored window cleaning gig at The Shard?"
The Mayor could see the wheels turning, he watched for a sign of life, a flicker of intelligent repartee to be delivered by those to whom such wit is, alas, not present.
"Not London," said Wottle.
"We only operate in Crewdley," added Daub, "we get a better response."
"Boys," said the Mayor, "be here tomorrow at ten o'clock. I might have something for you."
"You mean a Licence?" asked Wottle.
"No!"
"Oh! Ok then ... 'til tomorrow then," Daub said with some optimism.
"Forget the Performing Arts," the Mayor told them, "it's not for you."

*

At ten o'clock the next morning, Robespierre led Wottle and Daub into the Mayor's Parlour.
"Sit down," said the Mayor – they did. "Robespierre," he added "we shall have four cups of tea – off you go."

The Mayor did his best at small talk for the few minutes it took Robespierre to come back from the kitchen with a tray of four cups and saucers, sugar, spoons, milk and biscuits. They helped themselves.
"Right," said the Mayor, finally finishing his tea, "are you up for a spot of work?"
"Yes sir," Wottle said, "what's happening?"
"I want you two to watch a particular person in a particular property."
"Who? Which property?" asked Daub, having another biscuit.
"First of all," said the Mayor, "you must not breathe a word of this to another living soul –ok?"
"Yes!" they answered.
"Secondly, if you are seen doing what I ask you – again you are out. And I shall deny any knowledge of your activity. You'll probably get banged up for snooping, harassment and stalking. So don't get seen and don't get caught!".
"Who is it chief?" asked Wottle, "the big cheese? Lord or Lady Crewdley? Doc Scargreaves? The Town Clerk?"
"It's John Lacey! Do you know him?"
"Oh him," Daub said dismissively, "what's the big deal about him?"
"He lives up in the forest," Wottle declared, "you want us to watch him?"
"Yes," the Mayor answered, "could you do it?"
"Easy!" Daub declared, "we can hide in the trees and the bushes – in camouflage!"
"Well," the Mayor said "you already qualify with your choice of clothes. You look like two film extras from Jungle Jim meets Jenny Jungle."
"We can stay still for hours in one place," Wottle told him, "we go fishing on the river."
"I don't suppose you ever bother with a fishing licence?"
"It's the paperwork that trips us up Mr Mayor," Daub declared, "so we sort of blend in and keep quiet. The Warden doesn't see us. We can be by the river for hours – all night sometimes." "We keep very quiet", Wottle insisted, "unless the pollen gets up his nose. It makes him sneeze. Hay fever."
"It gets up my nose and makes me sneeze," Daub confirmed, "hay fever - even in January."
"Ah – that could be the start of a cold or the flu,", Wottle butted in, "it's freezing in the winter."
The Mayor had heard enough! "Gentlemen", he said, "I want you to watch John Lacey day and night – take notes - record every activity and anybody who visits him – got it! Report to meet every day at noon, or to Robespierre if I'm out – got it!"
"Yes Mr Mayor," Daub concurred, "what about our money?"
"Payment by results gentlemen! But one thing I can tell you is that it will be more than fourteen pence a week."
"Fair enough – how long for?" asked Wottle.
"Until further notice – until you give me information I consider to be useful enough for me to dispense with your services."
"Sounds fair enough," Daub added, getting to his feet.
"And I shan't be setting the Law onto you both for begging – or fishing without a licence – so go to it!"
The men walked slowly to the door, "can I take that biscuit?" asked Wottle.
"That's mine!" Robespierre said quickly, moving to take it.
Wottle and Daub left the Parlour. The Mayor watched as they walked out into Church Street.
"My God," he said, "compared to them Robespierre, you are a beacon of intelligence."
"Thank you Mr Mayor," answered the boy from the Bastille, "would you like the biscuit? It's chocolate – the Co-op's own make – great to dunk in your tea."

"Be quiet Robespierre – don't get above yourself" the Mayor said as he took the biscuit.
"And I suppose you have figured out what I want you to do?"
"Wash up the cups?"
"No! I want you to watch them."
"But Mr Mayor ...."
"No buts...."
"They will be hiding in the forest!"
"Precisely! And I want you to make sure they stick at it. They're the two biggest dopes in town."
Robespierre was bemused, "So why did you give them the job?"
"Because they're cheap," the Mayor answered, "and very, very simple. A bit like you really. Except you have had the benefit of working for me for thirty years and therefore have no doubt picked up a few useful attributes and altogether increased your intelligence to display the characteristics which make you what you are - loyal, dogged and rather well used to what it takes for me to survive and provide for us both."

"When do I go?" asked Robespierre, fully knowing the answer.
"Now!" the Mayor said, "so hop it, I've got things to do. Come back here late this afternoon. You should have the picture by then – five o' clock."
"Yes sir," Robespierre answered dejectedly, "will go."

*

Chapter 6

Robespierre cycled up towards "Cider Cottage" and parked his bike in a patch of ferns. He stooped, then crawled to get a good view of his quarry. Fifteen yards ahead he saw Wottle and Daub lying on their backs looking up at the sky. Wottle rolled over and looked towards "Cider Cottage."

"Nothing happening," he said rather quietly, but just loud enough that Robespierre heard.

"Waste of time," mumbled Daub.

"Precisely," Robespierre whispered to himself, gently removing a fern from down the collar of his shirt.

Suddenly a large van pulled onto the front yard of "Cider Cottage."

Wottle and Daub sat up. Robespierre could see they were covered in bracken and leaves in their attempt to remain inconspicuous. The three men watched as the driver got out and opened the rear doors. Two other men got out – Luigi and Salvatori. They went inside the cottage and Robespierre watched as Wottle and Daub resumed their horizontal positions.

Robespierre waited for another two hours. He looked at his watch – four thirty. He went back to where he'd left his bike. It wasn't there. He scrambled around in and out of the bushes and the thick undergrowth leading into the forest.

Just then, a frightening, lumbering beast ran right out in front of him – massive antlers hitting the lower tree branches, pelt as grey as the bark on the trees. It roared, and stood stock still to look at Robespierre.

"Mr Wooly!" said Robespierre, for indeed it was the Vicar of Crewdley doing what he often did between Church services, baptisms and burials, "what are you doing?"

"I'm a King Stag," answered the Vicar, "I'm rutting! I'm calling the herd together!"

"The Mayor will have to be told," Robespierre declared, still a little frightened lest the King Stag charged him and impaled him with the fearsome antlers.

"I don't care about him," the Stag roared, "this is my forest. I'm the King Stag around here. He's got about as much status around here as a fox or badger - no! I'm wrong! - a grey squirrel – that's what he is. And you are a toad Robespierre, so sod off back to Crewdley. Can't you recognise my status here in the forest? I'm the leader of the pack."

"Oh dear," said Robespierre, "I don't think you're going to be taking Sunday worship this week Vicar – you're not well in the head."

"Peasant!" the Vicar called as he hoofed it into the undergrowth.

"Did you steal my bike?" Robespierre called out. But the Vicar was gone.

"The English," Robespierre scoffed, "all mad."

*

It was five pm , and at Crewdley Town Hall the Mayor called the Property and Environment sub-committee to order. He wasn't happy of course, because Robespierre had not appeared at the instructed time.

"Right!" said the Mayor, "this meeting is underway – apologies!"

"Councillor Mrs Olivia Bland might not make it," said Councillor Morton Muggeridge, "she's sowing lettuce seeds. She'll try to get along later."

The Mayor was not impressed and let out an exasperated sigh in annoyance.

"Minutes of the last meeting – agreed?" he asked.

"Agreed," Muggeridge confirmed.

"Agenda item three – items requiring action," said the Mayor, "I've had a telephone request from Crewdley Environment Watch.

They want us to provide personnel to undertake a survey on the health of trees and wildlife in Crewdley forest."
"I nominate Olivia Bland," said Muggeridge.
"Don't be absurd. I've got two quotes here. The first is from Wildlife Action, a Birmingham Company that provided some trees for the Olympic Village - £4,000 plus accommodation costs."
"Next!" shouted Councillor Mrs Louise Evans Jenkins," I'm not paying that!"
"It's from a local Company - Crewdley Environment – two hundred and fifty pounds plus necessary equipment - butterfly nets, torches – that sort of thing."
"Agreed," the Councillors said as one, "Bloody cheek," said Arkwright, "those city cowboys think they can rip us off – well they can't!"

*

The next day, the Mayor got word to Wottle and Daub that they were to report to him at the Town Hall. Robespierre was present when the two stooges stumbled into the Parlour.
"Congratulations lads," the Mayor said insincerely, "you've been chosen to investigate trees and wildlife up in Crewdley Forest. You won the contract."
They were bemused, "We didn't put in for no contract," said Wottle.
"I did it on your behalf. You are now called Crewdley Environment Company. There will be a small fee – if you follow my instructions. Actually, there will be very little change in your activities. When you are up in the forest watching Cider Cottage, one of you write down notes about any trees you see that are diseased."
The boys looked extremely blank at the instructions, "Diseased trees," Daub mouthed without enthusiasm.
"And butterflies and birds – animals even. But just write it all down in a notebook and give it to me, Now – here's the clever bit, you can also keep another notebook and mark down the visitors to the cottage and the activities of John Lacey – got it?"
"Errm – could you just go over it again?" asked Daub.
"No it's ok," said Wottle, I think I've got it."
"So you are the brains of the team?" the Mayor said pointedly, "any questions?"
"No," Wottle answered, but Daub was not entirely at ease with the task at hand. "What about falling leaves? Does that count as diseases?"
Robespierre looked at the Mayor, who breathed in deeply and responded, "No – so well done with the Contract boys and keep me informed at all times – cheerio!"
They left the Parlour as if they were in a funeral cortege, sombre and without enthusiasm.
"You had better watch them in your free time," the Mayor told Robespierre, "I can't afford to have you charging around in the forest willy-nilly. I've got work for you here with me."
"Good news indeed Mr Mayor," Robespierre answered, "but I've something grim to tell you."
"Sharon Hayes has run off with the circus?" the Mayor added.
"No sir – the Vicar is running around the forest as the King Stag again. I ran into him yesterday."
"Yesterday! You should have told me straight away."
"I couldn't," said Robespierre, "somebody stole my bike. I had to walk back to town. That's why I missed your five o'clock deadline. I got back after six and you were not here."
"I was with Mrs Monroe," said the Mayor.
"Well – I had to go out myself."

"You spent the night with Sharon Hayes!" the Mayor accused.
"I'm here now Your Worship."
"Give me strength!"
"How about a bottle of Crewdley Blanc with garlic mushrooms and a nice omelette?"
"Get to it!" the Mayor concurred, then added, "are falling leaves a disease?"
"No your Worship."
"Quite! But that man hasn't got a clue."
"No sir! So why did you give them another job?"
"Because I'm desperate. I've got to find out what goes on at "Cider Cottage."
"They press olives," Robespierre interjected.
"I know that, but there's more," the Mayor affirmed, "I need information and I need it quick."
"Why?" asked Robespierre, pouring the first two glasses.
"Because the Flacks and the Italians are a threat to the democratic foundations of this town."
Robespierre drank from the glass and said, "Why - are they standing for Council?
"It remains to be seen," answered the Mayor, – "what the hell am I going to do with the Vicar? Mrs Wooly will freak out when I tell her."
"So don't tell her," suggested Robespierre.
"Omelette," instructed the Mayor drinking deep and topping up his glass, "and put some sliced beetroot in - and asparagus."
Robespierre walked through to the kitchenette and began to cook. The smell wafted into the Parlour, the Mayor lit a Cuban cigar. The smoke circled around his desk, the garlic mixed with it. "Mmm," he purred, "that's better."

*

This time, the Reverend Wilfred Wooly had definitely disgraced himself good and proper. It wasn't merely the King Stag display in Crewdley Forest – that had happened on numerous previous occasions. This time – he had not returned home. People were beginning to talk. Mrs Wooly did what she usually did and booked a month at The Vasco da Gama Hotel in Monte Gordo, Portugal.
So the only person left at The Vicarage, was the Town Clerks peculiar brother, Rupert Beard, tepee squatter in the garden, a man equally eccentric as the Vicar.
But the prime task was to capture Wooly and return him home. After that he would have to be kept under lock and key, with very close daily scrutiny, until the full moon had eclipsed and all thoughts of stags had been swopped for his church duties.
The Mayor considered his options, which weren't great. Wooly had to be caught, and the public must be kept in the dark. The police were out of the question, as were keen and trustworthy members of his congregation – none of them could keep their mouths shut at the best of times, and this wasn't even the best of times.
"Robespierre!" he called, "bring those clowns in the forest to me here now."
Robespierre was at attention and rocking backwards and forwards, even standing tip-toe in eager expectation of discernable instructions. But that wasn't discernable.
"Which ones? There are so many, "he proffered.
"Wottle and Daub you idiot!"
"I don't have my bicycle."
"So borrow one!"
"Who from?"

"Go to the Vicarage – here take the key. Take the Vicar's. It's in the shed – vamoose!"
Robespierre did as he was told and let himself into the Vicarage.
He walked through the empty rooms and out into the garden. He saw Rupert Beard's tepee, but chose not to disturb the man – if he was in situ. Robespierre looked at the original stocks on the grass and shuddered when he thought of the Flacks and the Crewdley Witch Trials of the 1640's.
"This place is mad," he said walking quickly to the shed to take the bike. He pulled it outside onto the grass and looked at it properly. It was no earlier than the 1960's and no later than 1980.
"What a wreck," he cursed, walking it back through the house and into the street.
He mounted up. It would be a long, arduous ride, up along Dark Street and uphill to Crewdley Forest.
"English idiots," he said as he peddled, "why me?"

*

Dorothy and Myrtle Flack were in the Wool Shop tidying up. "Brittany is doing so well, isn't she?" said Dorothy, "she really has taken to our new little business."
"No so little," Myrtle corrected her sister, "did you see last week's takings? Several thousand pounds."
"Yes", said Dorothy, "all that fruit and veg and flowers, and wine and cider."
"All local produce!" Myrtle added, "except the oranges, lemons, olives, bananas, pineapples etc, etc, etc."
"We do sell some good carrots and potatoes though – and lettuce and cabbages, beans, beetroot etc, etc, etc," Dorothy affirmed, "excellent produce – very local, very tasty."
They each took up their knitting needles and began to knit.
"We could always open another shop," said Dorothy.
"Why risk a winning formula?" Myrtle countered, "it's all working so well. I would be very reluctant to take on another shop, particularly in Crewdley. It's a small place."
"Maybe Kidderminster then, or Worcester?" suggested Dorothy. They looked at each other as their needles clicked and the balls of wool were pulled up sharply to allow more knitting. "No," they said as one.
"We're doing very nicely indeed thank you," Myrtle chipped in.
"Ah!" said Dorothy, "wise words." They spotted Claws on the shelf.
"There's a good cat," said Myrtle. "He's a good mouser," said Dorothy.
The cat watched the balls of wool as the women tugged at them after every row of knitting. Claws got off the shelf, jumped onto the carpet and lay in front of the heater.
"Let's have a glass of wine," Dorothy suggested.
"Oh yes – good idea," Myrtle concurred, "let's have a bottle of Luigi and Salvatori."
They did, and to round off the evening, after putting the "Closed" sign on the shop door, they each had a few glasses of "Forest Cider."

*

Two hours later, Robespierre, Wottle and Daub knocked, and were called into the Mayor's Parlour.
"I want you two to catch the Vicar," he said, "he's up in the Forest. He's had a nervous breakdown. Bring him back here pronto."
"How do we catch him?" asked Wottle, "how do you know he's still in the Forest?"
"He's got form," the Mayor told him, "he's up there all right."
"What about the trees survey?" Daub asked, "we'd already counted to forty seven then Robespierre collared us. He made me lose count."
The Mayor gave a sarcastic grin. "Next time take a few sticks of chalk. Put the numbers on the trees."

"Right," said Daub, adding quickly, "got any chalk?"
"Get some from the Co-op," the Mayor replied, giving the man a £5 note, "and get some shampoo. You look like an escaped orang-utan.
"Mr Mayor," Robespierre said, "how will they actually bring Mr Wooly into Crewdley?"
"In that wreck of a van they call a service vehicle, "the Mayor answered, "bring it round the back of the Town Hall and then bring Wooly up here to me. You go with them Robespierre. And I don't want any mistakes. Just imagine you are a hit squad with one objective – capture the Vicar – off you go! I shall be here waiting. You should get him easily – a few hours at the most."
The three men looked at the Mayor. They weren't happy. He pointed to the door and they went out.

*

The three hunters were driving in the van towards the Crewdley Forest. Robespierre was in the back. He reflected on how he had got there and wasn't happy. Wottle pulled into a clearing in the Forest that was quite near to "Cider Cottage." They got out.
"We'll walk into the Forest and wait," said Robespierre.
"Ah!" said Daub, "I can take the opportunity to count a few trees. I've got some chalk now."
Robespierre wondered exactly what made this man tick. He had no idea. He knew it would be useless to explain how they needed to be still if they were to surprise the Vicar and catch him. So he merely said, "You'll have to crawl in the undergrowth and mark the tree without standing up."
"I'd prefer to stand up," said Daub. "You can't!" said Robespierre, "the Vicar will see you and run off."
Daub considered his options. "Oh!" But I wanted to see the numbers on the trees when I was walking round."
"Ok – so after we've caught the Vicar you can come back and chalk the numbers higher up."
No reaction, but then Wottle said, "Ok let's get on with it. Daub – you go and crawl about over there – quietly. Mr Robespierre can sit down in these ferns and keep a low profile, eh Mr Robespierre?"
"Absolutely," the Mayor's man answered, "what else would we be doing up here?"
So they took up their positions. Robespierre could see Daub crawling around marking trees with yellow chalk.
"Your friend is persistent," he said to Wottle.
"Oh, he's persistent all right. He sticks at it. It's his best feature – persistent, yes that's what he is."
And so it went on, the search for the Vicar and the chalking of tress. After an hour of watching squirrels and birds, Robespierre suggested they move on. They wandered about in the Forest, not knowing where they were. Robespierre could see traces of sunlight coming through the tree-tops, but it didn't help. It was all very well knowing that the sun sets in the West. But where the heck were they? And then, through the trees, Robespierre saw "Cider Cottage," "Ok", he said, "we might as well stay here."
So they settled down and watched – birds and squirrels. Daub crawled about chalking numbers on trees, Wottle began to eat a sandwich and Robespierre drank whisky from a hip flask.
Suddenly, as if from nowhere, the Vicar moved quickly through the undergrowth towards the cottage.
"There he is," Robespierre said quietly.
"Let's get him," said Wottle.
"Wait!" Robespierre told him, "he's going to the back door."
The Vicar went straight into the cottage. "He went in!" said Wottle, how about that?"
"Ok," said Robespierre, "there's two doors to that place. Tell your mate to go stand guard at the front door. We'll go in after him through the back."

As Robespierre's words came out, he realised what he had said. It was never for him to play the hero, but needs must when the Devil drives. They ran to the back door.
"Now what?" asked Wottle.
Robespierre hesitated – but he knew what the Mayor would want him to do.
"We'll go in," he said firmly.
So Wottle turned the door knob and they stepped inside. The Vicar was sitting in front of the wood fire in the grate. "What's this?" he asked in shock, "What do you want Robespierre?" This is my free time away from church duties."
"The Mayor wants to see you," answered Robespierre, "now!"
"Not a chance," the Vicar replied, already hanging on to the arms of the chair as if his life depended on it. The cottage was gloomy, the windows were small and already a candle was flickering on the table. Robespierre focussed his eyes into the corner shadows. He saw another table. He was shocked to see piles of money on it. He turned his head over towards the staircase. On the floor were open boxes of jewellery. Nearby on the wall were oil paintings and on the window sill were statuettes. He looked all around and saw Wottle with his mouth wide open.
"Aladdin's cave," said Robespierre, "all that money! Where's it from?"
"Nothing to do with me," said the Vicar as he sat tightly to the chair. His stag skins were hanging to the floor. He had already taken off his antlers.
"I just use this place as a bolt hole – sod off!" he cursed them, "I'm not coming back and that's final!"
"It looks like a bank job," Wottle spluttered, "he's got some valuable stuff here."
"Not guilty!" declared the Vicar, "you need to speak to Mr Lacey. My relationship with this place is strictly one of a social nature."
"Grab him!" shouted Robespierre. Wottle did as he was told. Robespierre ran to the front door and told Daub to get inside. "Got the rope?" asked Robespierre.
"Yes sir," Daub replied.
"Tie him up then," Robespierre instructed him.
"You can't do this to me!" the Vicar shouted, "I'm in a private property!"
"Use the gag!" Robespierre yelled, "I don't want to hear a Vicar swearing. That would be completely beyond the pale – even for the English!"
So Wottle and Daub trussed him up like a chicken, then carried him outside and put him into the back of the van.
"You drive Mr Daub," Robespierre shouted, "we'll go in the back with the Vicar."
And so it was that the van pulled into the parking area behind the Town Hall. Wottle and Daub carried the Vicar up the stairs and Robespierre led them up to the Mayor's Parlour.
"Ah! Well done lads!" the Mayor said, "set him down and keep the gag on."
"Mr Mayor!" said Robespierre, "we caught him in "Cider Cottage."
"Oh! And what was he doing there?" The Mayor asked.
"It's his bolt hole," answered Robespierre, "but – there were things in the cottage that shouldn't have been there."
"What sort of things?" the Mayor asked.
"Oil paintings," replied Robespierre, "statues, jewellery and - piles of cash."
"Lots of it," Wottle concurred, "it looked like the proceeds of a robbery – maybe from a bank."
The Vicar was struggling to speak and get free from the rope. The Mayor took the bandage from his mouth.

"Nothing to do with me!" he blustered, "let me go home!" The Mayor put the bandage back on.
"Now listen to me," he said, "Winifred has gone to Portugal. Your flock is concerned about you. You've let everybody down – again! Robespierre – go get Doc Scargreaves."
"Yes sir!" and off he went.
Ten minutes later, the Doctor came and gave the Vicar a shot of something powerful, which immediately put him to sleep.
"Right you two," the Mayor said to Wottle and Daub," take him to the Vicarage and stay with him – put him in the wheelchair in the Foyer. When he wakes up – do not let him out – got it?"
"Yes sir," said Wottle, "but I need a pizza."
"I'll get one sent to the Vicarage – on the house."
They vacated the Parlour, but Daub's aroma lingered. "Would anybody like to tell me what's going on?" the Doctor asked, "it's been a long day and I'd like to go home."
"The Vicar has lost it again," the Mayor told him, "perhaps you could go round and see him tomorrow?"
Scargreaves got up from the chair, closed his bag and exhaled loudly. "This place gets worse," he said, "why don't they just transfer the old boy or pension him off? Do you know, the other week, he ran in front of my car on the Forest Road? Nearly hit him."
"Pity you didn't," said Robespierre.
The Doctor made his exit and the Mayor turned to Robespierre. "Pour the wine – get the oven on! Garlic mushrooms, truffles, fried eggs and a baked potato! I need to give all of this some serious thought." He lit a Cuban cigar and put his feet up onto the desk. Robespierre gave him a chilled glass of Crewdley Blanc. "Did Daub carry on marking the trees with his chalk?" the Mayor asked.
"Yes sir,"
"Thought so – absolutely no comprehension about the bigger picture. He hasn't got the brains of a bat!"
Robespierre grinned, "Was that a short – eared one or a cricket bat?"
"Shut it – pour me another drink!"

*

In the early hours of the next morning, the Mayor lay awake in bed, considering his options. Wooly was a hopeless case. But he would have to go in his own time, lest he confessed everything he knew about social life in Crewdley. A man like him gets to know many secrets. The trouble was for the Mayor, that some of them undoubtedly would lead back to him. Scandal had to be avoided at all costs. Yes, the Vicar might still divulge all he knew, even if his retirement was blessed by the Archbishop of Canterbury and his name was praised from every pulpit in England.
But if he were sacked – defrocked before his time – Wilfred Wooly would cause big trouble. The best course of action was to keep things as they were – as mad as they were.
One overwhelming force dictated that the status quo should endure. Winifred Wooly was that force. To upset her would be a disaster.
The Mayor turned over and considered how the Vicar's wife had scooted off to Portugal to let these difficult issues take their course.
"Wise woman," he mumbled, and went back to sleep.

*

Chapter 7

Harold Presbyterian, Mayor of Crewdley and its undoubted First Citizen, walked into Church Street and took in the air, partially poisoned as ever by traffic, but never the less, between the vehicles it was possible to breath in without exhaust fumes getting into his nose, throat and chest.

He looked across to the Mercian Bank and then to the Flacks Wool Shop. He took a few more steps and looked again at the Flacks "Fruit and Veg and Flower Emporium".

He walked down towards the River Side East, past "Caspian House", home of his mistress, Pippa Monroe. But then he considered Mrs Croker. He was spoiled for choice. Round the block and back up into Dark Street. He heard a pig squeal, and knew Percy Fish was feeding Pogo. Down again and back up into the Parlour.

"It's as clear as a bell now what I have to do," he told Robespierre.

"Oh really?" said Robespierre," well sir, as ever, I wait your instructions."

*

During the "Cider House Cottage Incident," Robespierre had had the presence of mind to pick up one of the bank notes from the table – just one – but it was conclusive. At the appropriate time he had given it to Mayor – oh and a very small white jewel. The appropriate time had been during their last meal together. Between the wine and the garlic mushrooms, Robespierre showed his hand, which of course was clasped around the bank note and the white jewel. The Mayor had been very pleased with his man's initiative. In fact, he had given Robespierre a hundred pounds from the safe behind the framed picture of himself on the Parlour wall.

As ever, the Mayor had thought very seriously about his options before taking any action. The key, he thought, was that the bank note was in fact, a one hundred euro note. He had taken the white jewel to a Jewellers in Birmingham. It was a diamond worth several thousand pounds.

In short, the Mayor deducted that a) the Vicar had nothing whatsoever to do with the loot, b) Lacey's cottage was being used as a safe house and c) the Italians were smuggling money, diamonds and works of art into Crewdley on the lorries containing olives, lemons, oranges, fruit and veg of all kinds, wine, tobacco and ironically – sponges from the Mediterranean. These were particularly well favoured by the female literati and bourgeoisie of Crewdley – not great in number admittedly, but discerning, non the less.

The only remaining issue for the Mayor then, was to decide on a strategy. Ideally, it would result in the eviction from the area of Luigi and Salvatori. His thought turned to Mrs Croker and banking. What happened to the loot after it left Cider Cottage? It was hot money of course, and needed a place to cool off. A bank seemed a good option – unless it was to be used as pay – off for the gang or its wider associates. The Mayor decided against the latter proposition. He would approach Mrs Croker, explain the situation, and ask if she was up to inviting the Italians to use the Mercian as their local bank.

*

At the "Forest Hotel", the Mayor and Mrs Croker were enjoying dinner in a private room, well away from the gaze of the prying public. Robespierre had been told to collect them at 10pm.

"Lucinda – I'm going to confide in you," he told her softly but with a serious edge, "can I trust you?"

"Yes Harold," she answered, "you can trust me completely. After all, we are virtually a couple."

"Hardly that," he told her firmly and with the slight dread he always got when a woman was getting too close, "but I need to take you into my complete confidence."

"Rock on," she said.
Pardon?" asked the Mayor.
"Oh sorry Harold – it's just something I picked up from Brittany Baxter and Sharon Hayes."
"My God!" he said in fright, "you don't socialise with those two do you?"
"Well," she answered in her most friendly manner, "Crewdley is a small place. They are engaged – loosely - in the business sector of our little economy. Our paths do cross on occasion. But I'm sorry, I interrupted you Harold. Please carry on."
"It was just the thought of you having a relationship with those two young women."
"Only in the business sense," she said emphatically, "now please tell me what you were going to say."
At that point, the Mayor hesitated. He needed time to think. No – he'd come this far, he had to go on – but.
"Let's have the other bottle of wine," he said, still thinking.
He poured the wine. It was rather obvious that Lucinda Croker had already enjoyed rather more Crewdley Blanc than would be recommended by a tee-totaller.
He was stuck. He had no choice. All other options were futile. He had to get rid of the Italians. He had to stop the Flacks taking over.
"Contraband money and works of art are being stored in this town," he declared as solemnly as he could.
"Everybody knows that," she said, "it's common parlance."
"What!" he exclaimed, shocked again by Crewdley's most eminent banker, "do you mean to say it's common knowledge?"
"Of course it is! It's a small town."
"Yes I know," he spluttered, "but for goodness sake – it's political dynamite!"
"I'm not worried about that Harold," she said coldly.
"You ought to be," he chided her," it all comes down to politics in the end."
"What I'm concerned about is the effect on the Mercian Bank. You know what happened before Harold?"
"Could I ever forget?" he remarked, pouring more drinks, "it's the reason you are sitting here with me instead of Roland Jones."
"Please!" she said sharply, "don't mention that man's name to me."
"Sorry," he apologised. "Sorry, but tell me Lucinda, what exactly is common knowledge about stolen loot in the town?"
"The Italians," she told him, "they smuggle stuff in on their lorries. The Flacks are up to their necks in it all," then adding quickly, "I'm related to them you know – cousin by marriage – my dozy departed husband has a lot to answer for."
The Mayor breathed in deeply and could only exclaim, "Bloody hell Lucinda, you're not part of their coven are you?"
"Certainly not!" she snapped," I can't stand them – creepy old things. They make my blood run cold."
"Excellent news," the Mayor said warmly, "that's a load off my mind I can tell you. So what else have you heard about Italian smuggling and Flacks complicity?"
"Rumours mostly."
"Typical!" he said.
"But where there's smoke ....," she suggested.
"There's a huge fire!" said the Mayor.
"Quite," she agreed, "but people are saying that works of art are being offered for sale on the black market, and rare antiques."

“So the Flacks have put themselves up for auction,” he smirked, ...“sorry Lucinda – carry on.”
“And,” she said, hesitating for effect, “some of my customers have started trying to pass off Euros into their deposit accounts. And when they go abroad – the bourgeois ones of course, they want to swap Euros for Dollars. But no one seems to know where it all comes from. It’s just the rumour that Crewdley seems to have become Palermo – what do you know Harold?”
“I know where its all stashed,” he said.
“So tell the police,” she said firmly, “that’s their job isn’t it?”
“Well quite,” he agreed,” but I don’t think Crewdley cops are up to the job in question. And if the issue went to an outside force - the Met or heaven forbid – Interpol or the EU Police – well let’s just say Crewdley would be finished as a centre of democratic delight.”
“Your words not mine,” she smiled, “I see things around here rather differently. But let’s not go into that just at the moment.”
“Quite!” he concurred, “but you would agree, I hope, that such a financial and criminal scandal would be a disaster for our town?”
“Yes I would,” she agreed, “so what are we going to do about it?”

*

Chapter 8

John Lacey walked into the Mercian Bank with a bag full of money. He asked to see Mrs Croker and she took him into a quiet back room.

"Please sit down," she said politely.

"I've got a lot of money and I'd like to have another account with your bank," he said.

"What sort of account might that be?" Mrs Croker asked him, "deposit or high interest?"

John Lacey smiled cunningly and raised his eyebrows. "Well," he drawled, "which one would you suggest?" He pulled out piles of Euros and put them onto the table.

"I can't accept those Mr Lacey," she told him.

"Why not?"

"Where did you get all that money from?"

"I saved it up."

"In Euros?"

"I've been abroad – and saved up."

"Doesn't seem likely," she said, "but I asked you here today to discuss your account with us."

"What's the matter with it?"

"Nothing at all – I merely wanted to tell you about one or two of our new products."

"Products?"

"Yes – investment opportunities. Obviously, this requires very serious thought."

Lacey thought for a moment, then retaliated, "Well this is an investment opportunity."

"I did not expect you to come here today with that amount of money."

"Well I did."

"Yes you did. And I now have a dilemma Mr Lacey."

"What sort of dilemma?"

"I can't be certain where you got the money from."

"I told you," he repeated, "I've saved it up and I've been abroad."

"Sorry Mr Lacey, but it doesn't ring true."

"Ok," he said, "I'll go to another bank," already putting the Euros back into the bag.

"Now wait just a moment," said Mrs Croker, "if you can honestly say that is how you obtained the money – perhaps I could put it into your account."

Lacey stopped stacking the cash into the bag. "There's' more," he said, "and I've got some very nice antiques and works of art I'd like you to keep in your strong room safe. And I would give you a nice commission for your trouble – you could take half of this money – there's more, as I said. The same commission for you would apply every time I used your bank."

"Mr Lacey – I think you are treading on very thin ice."

"But the art work, jewellery and antiques would have to remain intact. I've got some business friends who would take it very badly if the Madonnas and religious artefacts went missing."

"Fifty per cent commission on every money transaction. You deal only with me – no one else - understood?" Mrs Croker's icy attitude told him she meant business.

"Understood," he said, now realising this was a woman who could deliver.

"Sign here," she said pushing a document across the desk. He signed. "I'll sort the details out later," she added, "how will you deliver the rest of your deposit?"

"I'll bring it in bags and cover the paintings with cotton covers."

“On second thoughts,” she told him, “I think you’d better come here outside business hours.”

*

The next morning before day break, Lacey parked his van at the side of the bank. Mrs Croker let him in and he brought in about a dozen packages, bags and obvious framed paintings.
They carried the deposits down into the strong room. Mrs Croker locked the heavy metal door and put the key back into her pocket.
“Sign here,” she told him, and Lacey signed another form. He made his exit, got back into the van and drove off.
Mrs Croker used her mobile phone for a local call. “Harold,” she said, “exercise one complete – see you at lunch time at “The Forest Hotel.”

*

The Mayor had summoned Wottle and Daub to the Mayor’s Parlour, Robespierre in attendance.
“You’ve both done extremely well so far,” he told them, “and now your current contract demands one final effort.”
“We haven’t been paid yet,” said Wottle, “we’ve got overheads you know.”
“You’re on benefits,” the Mayor snapped, “don’t be impertinent – so listen up.
On Friday night, you will be round the back of the Mercian Bank in your van. You will be let into the Bank through the side door by a person who shall remain nameless.”
“The man with No Name – like Clint Eastwood,” said Daub, “will he be wearing a big hat and chewing a cigar?”
“I’ll ignore that comment,” the Mayor told him, “You will follow this person through into the Bank and go down to the strong room. You will then collect various boxes, packages and pictures and take them quickly and quietly back to the van.”
“When do we get our money?” asked Wottle.
“When the contract is completed,” the Mayor told them, “so you put the goods into the van, drove it up into the Forest and park up one mile before “Cider Cottage” by the road – got that?”
“Yes” they said as one. “Then leave the van – and put the keys under the windscreen wipers,” the Mayor told them sternly.
“Ah!” said Daub, “and then we walk back into town!”
“Exactly!” said the Mayor, “I think you are learning all the time.” He paused for effect, “Ok – that’s it! Friday – be there.”
The men left the Parlour. “And guess who is going to be there to pick up the van at about 3am?”
“Oh dear,” said Robespierre, “I was hoping for a night in with Sharon.”

*

A few nights after the briefing, at 3am on Friday morning, Wottle and Daub pulled up in the van outside the Mercian Bank. The side door was immediately opened, “Come in,” said the figure dressed in black and wearing a ghastly Halloween mask which muffled the phantom’s voice.
The “Person With No Name,” walked them through the Bank, down the steps and into the strong room.
P.W.N.N opened the metal – barred gate and went inside with the men. Another door was opened, and in the dimmest of lights, Wottle and Daub saw many pictures and secured leather bags.
P.W.N.N then opened up another safe and took out bundles of bank notes, and dropped them into empty bags. “Right! Let’s go back up!” P.W.N.N. said quietly.

The three of them carried the goods up the steps into the ground floor, then down the corridor to the bank door.

"You go out and quietly open the van," P.W.N.N said to Wottle.

This he did, and they quickly put all the goods into the van. "Go!" said P.W.N.N and they did.

P.W.N.N went back inside the bank, closed the door, and changed into normal clothing. The bells of St Crewd's Church rang for the quarter hour past 3am. Somehow, the Flack's cat Claw's had got into the Bank, "meow ...... meow."

"Be quiet," said P.W.N.N, "go catch a mouse."

*

Wottle and Daub were conservatism itself driving up to the Forest. Thirty miles per hour at all times until they approached the 'cattle grid' sign. They stopped the van. Another P.W.N.N came out of the trees, dressed in a long black cloak, black hat and – yes indeed – a grotesque Halloween mask.

Wottle and Daub looked at the figure in the pale moonlight, put the keys on the windscreen under the wipers – and walked quickly away towards Crewdley.

"I didn't fancy arguing with him," Daub said, "he looked horrible."

Robespierre took the keys from the windscreen, got in the van, and took the mask off "English idiots," he cursed as he started the engine and pulled away quickly and overtook Wottle and Daub.

"He's got our van," said Daub, "we could have had a lift," as it started to rain.

"I think I preferred window cleaning," said Wottle, "let's face it, we are working very unsocial hours."

*

Robespierre parked up at the back of the Town Hall. He and the Mayor unloaded the goods into the basement strong room, then Robespierre drove the van towards Kidderminster, parked it by the Safari Park, and walked back to the Mayor's Parlour.

They had several glasses of Crewdley Blanc, then an early breakfast – scrambled eggs, toast, tea – more wine. And so to bed!

*

Chapter 9

It's a strange thing indeed when a bank robbery has occurred and no one knows that it has happened – well of course three people knew – the Mayor, Robespierre and Mrs Croker. Others participated but alas, Wottle and Daub were not quite sure what had happened.

The town seemed as normal – all was quiet. The Flacks continued operating their two businesses, as did the Mercian Bank. The only difference now was that the transfer of collateral had taken place without the Italians, Lacey or the Flacks knowing.

And then, one day, Lacey had a call from Luigi and Salvatori. They wanted to make a serious withdrawal from the Mercian Bank and Lacey would have to take care of business.

So Lacey went to the Bank and had a meeting with Mrs Croker. "Of course," she said, "let's go down and have a look and you can decide what you want to take out."

They went down the steps to the strong room and looked at where Lacey's deposits had been put.

"Oh dear," said Mrs Croker, "it seems that it's all gone – have you delegated somebody else to collect it?"

Lacey was shocked – couldn't believe his eyes, "Bloody hell!" he shouted, "where is it?"

"You mean it's not you who has had it all removed?" asked Mrs Croker.

"No!" he yelled.

"In that case Mr Lacey," said Mrs Croker, "you have been robbed!"

*

A week later "Cider Cottage" was put up for sale by auction at the Forest Hotel. The Mayor attended, as did many others. The cottage was bought by an anonymous successful bidder. John Lacey had disappeared before the auction. "Cider Cottage" remained empty over the subsequent months.

The Italians came back to Crewdley for one final sweep. But their business had been undermined. They had been robbed. They were searching for Lacey, but all that remained at "Cider Cottage" was the huge, stone cider press covered in squashed apples. Even Billy the donkey had gone, so they returned to Palermo.

*

The Flacks Emporium quickly ran out of goods and services. Luigi and Salvatori had turned off the tap. No lemons, no olives, no cider, no wine – no business. The Emporium closed just before Halloween.

So the Flacks sole business was once again the Wool Shop. Brittany was welcomed back and Sharon Hayes resumed her duties at 'The Star and Garter.' Robespierre was happier – at least he knew where she would be! And the Mayor now had two mistresses. He was content.

Percy Fish continued to hunt for truffles in Crewdley forest with Pongo the pig. He kept an eye out for the Vicar , but the King Stag had gone to ground.

The Vicar had been put under a very strict and disciplined regime by Mrs Winifred Wooly – until the next time he transgressed and slipped back into wanton Pagan adulation of all things Forest and the magic of nature and the magic of the animal kingdom.

*

"It's the end of an era Robespierre," the Mayor told him in the Parlour, "fortunately a very brief era. An interregnum some would call it."
"An idiot would call it, ' the Boy from the Bastille' quipped.
"You don't know what it means do you?" asked the Mayor.
"No sir and I don't want to know. I've never heard the word before and I'd rather not ever hear it again. It's not the sort of word used in 'The Star and Garter.' I could hardly say - interregnum to Sharon, could I?"
"Oh shut up! What I'm trying to say is we are back to normal."
"Nothing is normal around here," Robespierre said.
"Point taken Robespierre – pour the drinks!"

*

The Flacks were sitting in their parlour knitting.
"It's funny how the Italians just disappeared," said Myrtle, "and that Mr Lacey."
"Yes," agreed Dorothy, "I'm not knitting anymore Italian football shirts for the Crewdley Teddy Bears."
"No," agreed Myrtle, "shall we do do more English?"
"Naw," said Dorothy, "let's do some Halloween pullovers."
"Oh yes!" said Myrtle, perking up, "and a few Bat, Cat and Cobweb Balaclavas!"
"And Witches on Broomsticks!" yelled Dorothy, "the kids will love 'em!"
"We could wear them and go for 'Trick or Treat!" Myrtle exclaimed loudly. And they did!

*

The Mayor had numerous complaints, but the season ended before the Flacks had been given the red card.
"What a ghastly prospect," the Mayor said to Robespierre, "Trick or Treat with them dressed as Witches and a carrying broom sticks."
"Please Mr Mayor," said Robespierre, "don't go there. It's too awful!"

*

It was the Christmas holiday period of 2013. The Mayor was looking out of the Parlour window down into Church Street. Wottle and Daub were cleaning windows. They had given the Mayor the useless information concerning the flora and fauna survey. He had given them £100 each. They were happy with that.
Wottle and Daub remained in the dark about the bank job. They didn't suspect Mrs Croker, but she had been the masked figure at the bank at 3am who had let them in and helped them load the van.
They also had no idea who the bizarre Halloween ghoul was (Robespierre) who had waited by the cattle grid in the forest at 3.30am and driven away in their van.
Daub was up the ladder cleaning windows. Wottle had a foot on the bottom rung. They were still talking about the bank incident.
"Nothing was ever reported," Daub called down, "but who were those two people in the masks?"
"I don't know," Wottle shouted back. Some things are best left unknown if you ask me. Put it down to experience. Nice little hundred quid each though 'eh?"
The Mayor continued to look down into the street. "Robespierre," he said, "I think we got away with it!"

"Yes sir," he replied, "there's still talk at 'The Star and Garter' about Lacey – and the Flack's Emporium closing. People say it was all down to the Italians pulling out."
"And so it was," the Mayor answered, "but we know exactly why they pulled out. And that's the secret of my success. Plan ahead Robespierre. Work it all out before you strike a blow."
"Mrs Croker knows", said Robespierre.
"Of course she does. She was key to the whole operation. I couldn't have pulled it off without her. Why do you think I seduced her in the first place?"
Robespierre was unmoved, "Mr Mayor," he said, "can you really rely on her?"
"Can I really rely on you?"
"Yes sir," Robespierre answered.
"It was a rhetorical question," said the Mayor.
"Rhetorical," Robespierre repeated, " interregnum .... indeed Mr Mayor. I know rhetorical and I looked up interregnum. So here's one for you .... which town was called 'Spooksville' in a 19th Century Folk story?"
"No idea Robespierre – tell me!"
"Crewdley," he answered, "it was a story about ghosts and gouls, written by one of the Flack's ancestors."
"Typical!" said the Mayor, "I'm surprised this town has survived for so long with the Flacks being here."
"Well sir," said Robespierre, "I think they're here to stay."
"They don't have children – their line will die out!" the Mayor snapped.
"No sir!" said Robespierre, " the Flacks have adopted Brittany Baxter and she's pregnant."
"Oh my God!" said the Mayor, "it's Salem all over again."
"You don't have children," Robespierre chided him.
"Neither do you!" the Mayor answered.
"I'm going to get hitched to Sharon Hayes," Robespierre declared, "we could have kids."
"Well I've got two women who could be interested," the Mayor boasted, "and do you know what Robespierre? I'm going to take up the challenge. You're quite right to have raised this issue. Now – garlic mushrooms and fried eggs if you please!"
"Coming right up," replied Robespierre.
"I'll do the drinks," the Mayor told him, "then let's get the women round here."

Robespierre stopped in mid stride, "Sir", he said, "surely not in here."
"Why not? It's about time I made a few decisions about my descendants."
"But sir .... it's unlike you to act in a rash manner."
"Time waits for no man – or woman," the Mayor declared pouring the drinks, "I'll try Mrs Croker first, she's younger."
"She's not as young as Sharon," said Robespierre.
"Neither is Lady Gaga," the Mayor told him, "get the frying pan on!"

*

INTERMISSION

To be continued